Praise for
Based on True Stories

Matt Potter's writing voice possesses a delicate snark, an incisive wit that lifts even the commonplace into unique memorability. The characters who saunter – sometimes wander, sometimes traipse – throughout this collection of bite-sized fiction have the makings of great fictional people: they're singular and quirky, but somehow, at the same time – and here's where my admiration for Matt's skill goes off the chart – they're possessed of an indisputable sense of reality ... These people exist, they live and breathe, and we, the readers, recognize in them our friends, our family ... And ourselves.

~ Guilie Castillo Oriard, author of *The Miracle of Small Things*

Real characters with real conundrums. Coarse, flawed and lovable. Potter's stories are written with a healthy portion of humour and humanity.

~ Michelle Elvy, editor, *Flash Frontier: An Adventure in Short Fiction*

The small fictions in *Based on True Stories* will not lull you – they will piss you off or, at the least, move you to indignation, or tears, or laughter. Maybe all three. These gems provoke, like the tip of a chef's knife pricking skin, and just as the words get uncomfortable, the story delivers the bit of redemption that reveals the humanity of his characters – and of us all. These stories are real, raw, and honest. The reading doesn't get much better than that.

~ Linda Simoni-Wastila, Senior Fiction Editor at *JMWW*

also by Matt Potter

all you need is ... a whiteboard,

a marker and this book!

Books #1 and #2

(Everytime Press, 2016)

Hamburgers and Berliners
and other courses in between

(Červená Barva Press, 2015)

Vestal Aversion

(Pure Slush Books, 2012)

BASED ON TRUE STORIES

Matt Potter

TRUTH SERUM PRESS
Adelaide, Australia

First published as a collection March 2016

ISBN: 978-1-925101-75-1

Truth Serum Press
4 Warburton Street
Magill SA 5072
Australia

Email: truthserumpress@live.com.au
Website: http://truthserumpress.net
Truth Serum catalogue: http://truthserumpress.net/catalogue/

Front cover photograph copyright © fcl1971
Author photograph copyright © Paul Beckman
Cover design by Matt Potter

Also available as an eBook
ISBN: 978-1-925101-76-8

for

the woman in orange

at Jungfernstieg S-Bahnhof

Contents

Friday

Entertainment Land

Morgana Malone and ...

Volumes

Sex and Love

The World According to Trudy Polaris

Commuting

FRIDAY

The *Friday* stories were written for my Featured Author stint on *Pure Slush*, in February 2013.

The central incident really happened, in a café in the Adelaide Hills suburb of Blackwood. But despite searching and local publicity surrounding the case, I could not find out why ...

So I invented a reason.

I had long wanted to write a backwards story, or rather a story where the action is told backwards, and this story provided the right vehicle. Because the real story here isn't what happened, but why. And we find out why as we journey back in time.

The
Never Far From Home Café,
Friday, 1:57pm

And I'd even put on lipstick and tied my hair up in a bun!

"Waddaya want for your soundbite?" I asked them, sounding professional, squinting at them with one eye because I was looking into the sun, standing where the gum trees used to be because the Council cut them down out the front of the café only last week. "I can give you anything."

'Course, they cut that bit out.

If you were watching the six o'clock news on TV, all you saw was the outside of the café and the reporter talking to the camera and some jokers in the background looking like they were part of the action, like at a car race or the Christmas Pageant. All you saw of me was me saying, "It all happened in a split second. She just stood up and poured the tea over his head. I didn't see any of it." And there I was squinting into the sun again.

This is what I saw. They were all sitting at tables in the window, but she had her back to the two guys. Normally she sits where they were sitting, she comes in every day but I've never seen them before. So maybe that pissed her off. The guys were wearing uniforms, dark blue shirts with white trim and Kuhlschrank and Sons Funerals near the pocket, so maybe that had something to do with it too. The funeral home is just around the corner and it's an old neighbourhood so they get a lot of business.

I heard a loud voice and I looked up from sprinkling cheese across a Napolitana pizza roll and saw it was her. "Do you mind?" she was saying. "I'm trying to eat my lunch in peace." Just like that, kind of like an opera singer, her voice going up and down. I thought she was joking, but when she flicked her hair out – it's long and dyed brown and looks like straw – I could see oh, she meant business. "Could you move, please? Your conversation is upsetting me," she said. She said it sort-of looking away, over her shoulder.

But they stayed in their seats.

It was lucky I saw what I did because Marjorie who's manageress here at the Never Far From Home Café has problems remembering things and can't even remember if she spreads butter on bread for a sandwich.

(We use that cheap caterers' blend margarine that looks really pale when you spread it on white bread, and 'cos her eyesight is so bad too, she can't see it. She has to taste it to check, so unless you're happy to have your sandwich a bit discounted with a bite taken out of it, get me to make it for you. Though she's not a big eater so it's just a small bite.)

Yeah, but the lady pouring the tea over the young guy's head? Never said a cross word to me ever so I don't know what upset her.

Earlier

"Could you move, please? Your conversation is upsetting me." She turned around again and spooned more salad roll into her mouth.

I laughed. A spoon?!

She looked at us like she was a crossing guard. And we were twelve. And we had stepped off the kerb before she'd stuck her STOP sign out for cars to stop.

Jarred shook his head and turned around to look at her. She had on the white shirt she wears every day and she flicked her bad dye-job hair. I'd never heard her voice before.

"Nobody's making you eavesdrop, darling," Jarred said.

She looked over at the woman behind the counter, the one with cross-eyes, and opened her mouth. But cross-eyes was busy.

"I was here first," she said, turning towards us again. "I come here every day and I always sit at that table." And she pointed to the table where we were sitting. "And I sit in that seat." And she pointed to the seat where Jarred was sitting. But she didn't point at Jarred, just the chair. "I was ordering my lunch at the counter, and you came in and sat down. Where I always sit."

"You're the one not happy with the musical chairs, sweetie," Jarred said. "If you don't like our conversation, leg it, love."

She touched the cross resting on her shirt. "I am tired of your gutter talk," she said, not looking us in the eyes. "I'm a Christian woman and I don't have to listen to your disgusting conversation."

Jarred raised his eyes. Like he was praying for relief. "You getting your jollies listening to us talk about what we do away from work?" he said.

"I come here for quiet," she answered, standing up, "for sanctuary, and to listen to your talk of –"

But she stopped, and sat down again with her back to us.

I looked at Jarred and Jarred pretended to spoon food into his mouth and I sniggered. "Those Christians know how to roll out the welcome wagon," he said.

She spooned more salad roll into her mouth and picked up her cup of tea and looked at the tablecloth pretending we weren't there but we were there, right behind her. Disgusting her with our presence.

"Makes me want to come here every lunchtime now," Jarred said. "Soak up the friendly atmosphere."

Her chair scraped on the floor tiles but I wouldn't give her the satisfaction of knowing I was looking. So the next thing I saw was her white shirt behind Jarred, and him saying, "Eeeewwww!" and I looked up just as she put the cup back down on the table. And Jarred's head was dripping.

"It's only lukewarm," she said. "They never make it very hot here."

Jarred sat there, grimacing, shoulders hunched over, not sure what she was going to do next.

She picked up her bag and her cardigan from the spare chair. "Some people need to learn some manners," she said. And walked out the door.

Earlier Again

When he flicked his lighter I grabbed his hand and cupping it in mine, leaned in. The cigarette stuck to my bottom lip caught the flame. And as the smoke puffed between us, just before I pulled away, I looked up at him – a split second – from under my eyelashes.

"Thanks," I said. But I couldn't see his eyes through his sunnies. I stood back, breathed out so my chest filled my one-size-too-tight Kuhlschrank and Sons workshirt, and blew smoke out across the car park. "So was he good?"

I didn't really want to hear the answer. A three-night-stand a year ago and I'm still making goo-goo eyes whenever Tony's name is mentioned. But I have this need to *know* ...

"Yeah."

"Did you fuck him?"

Tony shook his head and flicked ash into the rose bushes. "Thick cock," he said, holding his hands out, measuring the circumference. "Massively thick." And his fingers spread wider. "A real arse-splitter."

"Yeah?"

"Yeah."

"Well, you're walking around okay today," I smiled.

"Yeah, it was just what I needed." He stretched and yawned.

The side door of the vestry flew open. "Fellas," Brian said, eyes sliding. "I say this every day. Smoke over there." And he pointed to some bright asphalt.

"It's too sunny over there," I said.

Brian sighed. "This ... is ... a non-smoking ... zone."

We stepped a few steps away from the vestry, Brian finished his school principal wowser act and the door closed.

"Fuckin' uptight shit," I said. "Needs a good cock up his clacker to calm him down."

Tony laughed. I like to make him laugh. "You offering, Jarred?"

"Not a chance," I said. "That's old news, baby."

Tony smiled. Looked away. Flicked his cigarette butt into some more roses and shoved his hands in his pockets. When he does that, it's hard to know if he's playing with his cock or if he always smiles that way.

I looked down. My nipples stood erect against my blue shirt. "My hole needs a workout soon," I said. "It's starting to grow over."

"Go to the sauna," Tony said.

"Yeah, I might."

No flicker from him at all. Like I'm just there to take the edge off.

"Just lie back in a sling and take on all comers," I added. "I'll let them do all the work."

"Line 'em up."

"Yeah," I said. Thinking all I really want is for him to be the one lining up. "Get my hole fucked so hard it's gaping open but I've got a smile on my dial from arsehole to breakfast time."

"Yeah," Tony added, "so to speak."

I looked over at the building and saw a flash of white in a window. Then heard the *schtock!* of the window sliding shut.

"Hungry?" Tony asked, taking his hands out of his pockets, still smiling.

"Starving," I said, dragging on the end of my cigarette. "Could chase the horse and suck the rider."

"Good," Tony said. "Time for a late lunch."

Even Earlier Still

Their voices came through the window before I saw them. Then I spotted their blue shirts with the white piping – like many of the other staff here wear – but their conversation ...

Though today they were much later than usual.

I looked at my computer screen and blocked their voices out, stopped up my ears with the music I'd heard last night from the church choir.

Once, just once, I wish Brian wasn't so good at his job and would let them smoke their cigarettes closer to the vestry.

I shuddered as I pulled out the second drawer under my desk and placed my hand on the Bible resting inside. My fingers were light on the worn leather and I didn't even say a prayer, I just ... thought.

And wondered what *It's starting to grow over* means.

I didn't want to listen to their voices but they were *there*, on the other side of the open window, and I saw his face but I didn't want to remember that either.

Closing the drawer, I twisted my wrist to look at my watch: two minutes and I could leave. I'll have a salad roll, I thought. Which is what I have most days. The younger woman at the café makes the salad rolls. The older one forgets to put most of the salad in.

More laughter from outside. I moved the cursor to the bottom of the screen and with two clicks, logged out of my computer.

These men make me think of my son and what he is doing in his life now and I don't want to think of my son and the path he has chosen away from God.

I wondered if they know him and I pray, I pray they don't.

Get my hole fucked so hard it's gaping open but I've got a smile on my dial from arsehole to breakfast time.

I stepped around my desk and threw the vertical blind aside. Bible verses filled my head but their talk had left the words clogged in my throat. So I just slammed the window shut.

They didn't even turn to look.

Grabbing my bag and cardigan from the chair, I neatened my Wednesday blouse by pulling it down at the waist, smoothed my crucifix across the bustline, and straightened the collar. This blouse has tiny white cherries appliquéd on the collar points. I'm sure I'm the only one who has ever noticed them.

I pushed the slide next to my name across on the In Out board. I'm always the last to leave for lunch. Everyone else has finished it by the time I go.

Checking my reflection in the glass of the front door, I opened it to exit the building. I must add hair dye to my shopping list, I thought. And stepping out into the sun, wondered what drink would go best with my salad roll.

ENTERTAINMENT LAND

Duality and dual lives and the fakery that goes into leading lives in the public eye have long fascinated me.

Similarly, I am not so interested in war stories, but stories from the homefront – the stories behind the stories – are always of greater interest.

So these stories are about alternate realities and the lengths to which people go to maintain their own versions of reality and the lengths to which people go to make their lives more bearable and the lengths to which people go to get their piece of the action, however small the action or the piece might be.

Reality is, after all, in the eye of the beholder.

All these stories were written for *52 / 250 A Year of Flash*.

Pitcher

3D is killing my porn career.

So I stand at the end of my driveway wearing a matching white halter and latex micro-mini, pitcher in hand, selling homemade lemonade to drivers-by.

Traffic on the street has tripled since I started. Many drivers recognise me from *Squat and Cough 7*, my last big success. And there have been quite a few rear-end collisions too.

A frequent driver-by is Barney, my ex-husband.

"It's your fault I'm doing this, Barney," I screamed through the driver's window of his BMW as he pulled up yesterday.

"You got the house *and* the pool boy in the settlement," he yelled back.

"And you got the plastic surgeon!" Bending over, I had to hitch up my halter. "Now I can't go within 200 yards of his practice or house or mother!"

Never marry a divorce lawyer. And if you do, never divorce him.

Barney buzzed up the windows and I saw my tits in the dark reflection: sagging, especially around the edges.

I threw the pitcher at the car and smashed the window, lemonade and glass splattering everywhere. Tyres squealing, he sped off.

It's hard getting work done that's cheap *and* reliable, so sagging anything is a major career-crisis.

Tottering on my ten-inch wedges back to my lemonade stand, I imagined how many more glasses I'd need to sell before I can get my new super-size-me, gravity-defying rack.

As my career counsellor once said: Be proactive! If life hands you lemons, make lesbian porn.

Write

I pasted a sample paragraph of my writing on the website *Who do you write like?*

The response was immediate. I suddenly saw myself in long beard and flowing tunic, dispensing wisdom and loaves and fishes.

Switching off the computer, I caught my enigmatic smile on the blank screen.

My wife hurried past, holding an empty tray. "What're you smiling at?"

She disappeared, no time for an answer, door slamming.

I sat, considering this new enormity. I could found my own religion. Some man – prophet, seer, philosopher – develops a system of thinking and wham! they're building worship centres and theme parks and re-naming interstate highways after him.

Makes you think.

My wife hurried through again, tray stacked high with plates.

"I pasted a paragraph of my writing on the website *Who do you write like?* and it said I write like *The Bible.*"

She glanced as I followed her into the kitchen. She put the tray down, filled the coffee machine with tap water, spooned coffee into the two-cup filter, stamped it down with a grunt, snapped the filter holder into place, flicked the on-switch, and stood, waiting for the first hiss.

She looked me in the face. "So I guess you'll be starting your own religion, then?"

"Why do you say that?"

"Because I did the same thing and it said I write like the Dalai Lama, so I thought we should move to Tibet. Coffee?"

Normally I'm allergic to bullshit but sometimes it can be a sneaky bitch.

Ethics

Here's one I prepared earlier, I'd said. Please note the word *"earlier"*.

Still, the world runs on celebrity.

I was good-looking, marketable and ambitious. And that never hurt anyone cracking it big, even daytime big, the coveted 2:00 – 2:30pm timeslot.

And nobody seemed to notice only the guests did the actual cooking. Sure, I chopped, smiled at Camera 3, recommended sponsors' products: *These Chopperholic knives are great for chives. Nothing stirs custard better than a Stir-a-Durable frost-free spoon.*

Or gave hints: *It's all in the wrist*, and *Just like Great-grandma used to make, but without the indentured labour.*

So I was unprepared when making Overeasy Eggs Kilpatrick for Two – *Here's one I prepared beforehand* – and there they were, in the Unbelieva-steel frypan, still thawing inside their generic brand packaging.

Damn cross-promotional live demonstrations during the news hour.

(I also had new ill-fitting contact lenses and the steam from the toaster – I was using frozen bread – fogged them up. No wonder I didn't see that the Overeasy Eggs Kilpatrick for Two were still in their plastic packet!)

Celebrity Chef Can't Cook for Nuts! headlines said. Not true, I responded: I've always been a fan of mental illness.

They fired me but I sold my story to another network. They're hoping to revive – or recycle – an old genre by turning it into a TV Movie of the Week.

The contract states I must play myself. But I'm hoping they'll realise I can't act and pay me extra *not* to do the job.

Welcome to our community

"Yeah, she's a real slut," many contestants' mothers say.

"If he could only keep it in his pants, he'd probably be able to stay in the country," others say about their sons.

I sit in my beanbag, sipping beer and semi-flaccid, watching the new dating show *Loose Connections*, previewing it for a local community TV channel. I have to give it its correct classification. So I'm the one who decides which large letter flashes on your TV screen, and if you should send your kids out of the room now.

To become a contestant on the show, people you know have to answer a series of questions about you: this includes people you've had sex with, people who've watched you have sex with others, people from your church, and your parents. (It's a New Zealand production.)

Once you're on the show, it's downhill – or even further downhill – from there.

What sort of people will watch this new low in trash-TV? Sad fucks, that's who; people who have nothing better to do than sip beer late at night while lying in beanbags trying to muster the energy to rub one off.

I put my beer down and looking at my clipboard of guidelines, close my eyes and stab the page with my pen. *G,* for *general exhibition.*

OK, it's not a foolproof system. But I'm also on the station's Publicity Committee and being so far down on the dial, we need all the publicity we can get.

True Vocation

Clapping my hands against my cheeks, I shriek, then throw my arms around the chunky woman beside me. Screaming, we hug each other tight, jumping up and down.

"Amazing!" says Cherie. "Did you feel the *emotion*? Was it *real*?"

We nod, gasping for breath. My heart is pumping.

Cherie turns to the class. "*Great* pairwork! *Imagine* what that *feels* like with an entire *audience* doing it? It's *electric*!"

The class claps as we sit down again.

I smile. The four-week training course has boosted my self-confidence: no athlete or dancer or ninja is more dedicated.

A normal day begins with hair, make-up and wardrobe, then the gym for weight training and stamina building and the pool to cool off.

After lunch it's vocal coaching: shrieking, screaming, crying *Oh-my-God!-Oh-my-God!-Oh-my-God!*, panting and face-fanning. Next it's 'situational training', where we pretend to be audience members on real talk shows and practice everything we've learned that day.

Every Friday afternoon we're strapped into chairs and tests are run on our excitement levels. We're given a grade on sweat, tears and blood pressure and how much noise we make. (Thursday nights are practice practice practice.)

Rumour says we'll be tested on how we throw ourselves about, but I'm not sure how they'll do that: a padded room with sensors and a camera, maybe?

I start work experience soon. I get to sit in the audience of a real talk show. I'm working on getting so excited, I piss my pants.

Numberplate

My mother was never the happiest of people.

She turned to me one day, rubbish and other detritus piled high around her in the garage and said, "I want to give you this." It was a numberplate from a car. Just one.

I did not recognise the numbers, but took it gracefully and wondered aloud why she wanted me to have it.

"It has great sentimental value to me," she said, eyes misting. It was clearly painful for her to talk about, so I let it slide.

After she died, clearing out her safe deposit box at the local bank, I found more numberplates. There were ten, all polished and shining, just one each, not both to complete a set, and of different vintages. I had no idea she had ever collected them.

And with them was a brief letter, on which was written, *To be opened in the event of my death, Marion Slipkowiecz*, in her familiar scrawl.

My life has not been the best, often miserable, she had written on the paper. *But whenever I had a nice time, I would take the numberplate off a nearby car, as a memento.*

Perhaps you could track down the owners and give them back. They are the milestones of my life.

Of course I kept them. They hang above my desk, alphabetised and descending. I have no idea which happy moments they marked in my mother's life, but despite their minimum cheer, they oddly connect us.

MORGANA MALONE AND ...

Morgana Malone was created for *Pure Slush*'s 365-story project, *2014 A Year in Stories*. 31 writers from around the world each took the same day every month, and wrote a continuing story set on these same days. All were written in present tense, like the stories are unfolding now, as the readers reads them, like an episodic novella.

My day was the 25th of each month.

And I have always loved titles like *Nancy Drew and the Mystery of ...* or *The Hardy Boys and the Riddle of ...* (the ole *variation on a theme* idea though these stories themselves are not the sort I like to read, even as a kid) and so I wrote these twelve linked stories about Morgana Malone and her search for ... something.

The themes covered in these stories are all favourites.

Morgana Malone and the Case of the Mysterious Flood

Saturday, 25th January 2014

"You have no idea what you're talking about, do you?"

He's at it again. With five minutes of the gallery tour left, his voice still sounds from the rear of the twenty-plus group: soft enough for the old ladies in front not to hear, but insistent enough that I wait for his intake of breath before he speaks, and wince.

And I was hoping my new orange bob made me unrecognisable.

"You can see by the way the colours *pop* out at your eyes," I say, hand shaking at the picture throbbing on the wall, my apricot broderie Anglaise shoulder ruffle flapping against my upper arm. "It's a really eye-popping painting." I turn my head from the blue and yellow and green and purple and other ugly colour swirls and step towards the doorway.

"Nobody has any idea what she's saying," he says – to someone, anyone, no one, everyone, who knows: the old ladies have all turned away from him as far as I can tell. "She's talking into the ether and it sounds like Sanskrit. And that hair colour?" he snorts. "She looks like a carrot."

My heels clack on the parquet floor as I walk, through the large doorway and into the next gallery. I'd challenge him, if this wasn't my first day on the job. *Carrots used to be your favourite vegetable*, I'd say. And wait for him to deny it.

Perhaps becoming a volunteer gallery guide to meet men was not such a good idea.

(I'm so sick of bogus profiles on the internet! They all look great on the screen – *Me: down to earth, like people to be themselves, good sense of humour* - but then you meet them! Men worth millions still living with their mothers. Men who are 'single' betrayed by their wedding ring tan lines. Men who say, "I'm paying so much in child support I need to know how fertile you are," even before I buy them a drink.)

I clasp my hands in front of me as I turn on my high heels to face the group. Two old ladies stare, giving me their brightest attention.

"As you can see by the brilliant bas-reliefs above us on the ceiling, we're now in the original part of the Gallery." I clasp my hands tighter, to stop myself from gesturing towards the ceiling with shaky fingers, to keep my balance on my high heels.

Old ladies muster around me.

A guffaw sounds from the back of the group.

The bastard knows I've always hated my brown hair.

"This part of the Gallery first opened in 1882," I say, "and was built with a generous bequest from Sir

Farquhar McPherson, whose brother Sir Darymple McPherson made an equally generous bequest three years later, to match the original."

"What media were used to create the bas-reliefs?" He's standing off to the side now.

I look at him and see there's something different about his eyes: whitened, and flattened, like the wrinkles have been blasted off.

"They look incredibly unique," he adds, "or maybe even uniquely incredible, so I'm fascinated to know what they're made of." He smiles. "Can you inform us?"

I look at another older woman who stands, head cocked, waiting for my answer. A gold tooth glints inside her puckering mouth.

"Plaster of Paris, creek water and old egg cartons," I say, "all mooshed together in a big cauldron and slapped up there with large paintbrushes made of virgin horsehair." I smile, holding back a scream. "Thanks for joining me on this tour this afternoon. Please enjoy the rest of the Gallery."

I turn. My heels are brisk on the marble floor and as I pass him I smell his cologne, woodsy in that Eastern Bloc way I remember so well. "Don't follow me, Grigor," I say, "or I'll call Security."

Other voices disappear behind me. I walk through the next doorway, head down, heels clacking, and then through another door and then another door marked 'Staff Only' and down the stairs, clack-clacking my way to the toilets marked 'DANGER – subject to flooding'.

§

As soon as I hear the restroom door pushing open, my eyes flash to the latch. Unless he climbs over or under the cubicle walls or over or under the door or has a screwdriver to unscrew the lock or a gun to shoot the lock off, I'm safe sitting on the toilet lid.

The restroom door wheezes closed behind him. Knuckles rap hard on the cubicle door.

I hold my breath.

"What are you doing, Morgana? Why are you pretending to be someone you're not? As soon as I walked into the gallery and saw you standing by the *Guided Tours here* sign with your shoulders slouched and hugging your elbows like a street waif, I knew it was you. You can't hide behind that orange hair colour."

My eyes are wild in my head. "You have no right to come here, Grigor. This is for staff only." I answer with what I hope is strength and confidence.

(*But you're not staff, you're only a volunteer,* I expect him to say.)

"Your voice sounds weak and unconfident," he says. His signature Spanish sandals poke under the door and his voice sounds skewed, as if he's talking into the painted wood and his chest. "You need to come back to intensive therapy."

I look down at my shoes. Open-toed and two-tone peach and tangerine to match my hair, they're a mere school ruler-length away from touching the toes of Grigor's sandals and perfect for a January summer day except the closed heels rub raw under my ankle bones and they're so high any degree of nerves makes the balancing act –

"I have a free appointment at 9.30 on Monday," he says. "I can get Zebadie to block the time out in my schedule for you. I can call her now and get her to keep it free. I can do that if you want, Morgana." He shifts his weight and his sandals squeak on the marble floor. "I can do that for you right now. I can call her up and tell her it's an emergency and have you booked in for 9.30 Monday morning. It's as easy as that." I hear the rustling of fabric. "I'm getting my mobile out of my pocket now and calling Zebadie to make the appointment, even though it's a Saturday now. And you won't have to do anything but turn up at 9.30 on Monday. That's only two days away."

I cough to clear my throat. "I won't marry you to get discount therapy, Grigor."

"You won't have to this time," he sighs.

I shake my head.

His voice softens. "Things will be different this time."

I fold my hands in my lap. I have another thirty minutes before my next tour and after fifteen years in therapy with poor timekeepers, am pretty good at waiting.

"Please," he says.

I twiddle my thumbs, then breathe out, relaxing my spine and slouching against the cistern, my apricot broderie Anglaise shoulder ruffle now reaching down to my navel.

"I promise," he whispers.

I can't believe I say it, but I do. "What did you do to your eyes, Grigor?"

I hear a sharp intake of breath against the door. I wince.

"Just some light freshening up," he says. "They help me see better into people's psyches now the excess skinfolds are gone, so I have a much clearer vision and I'm really pleased with the result. Now my eyes look the way they were always meant to look."

I remember the mirror he kept behind the couch in his consulting room. He would watch his reflection while counselling patients about their body image issues.

Grigor's voice deepens again. "But that's really not important now, Morgana. It hasn't escaped my notice that you've dyed your hair the colour of my favourite vegetable."

I cross my ankles, but leaning back while perched on the toilet lid with crossed ankles doesn't work (unless I want to stretch out and touch toe-to-toe with Grigor) so I put my hands by my side, wrapping my fingers around the edge of the seat to steady myself. But the cold of the white porcelain is a shock to my fingertips so I sit up again. The toilet seat creaks.

"Are you constipated, Morgana?"

Standing up, I press the button. The sound of water splashing out of the cistern and into the bowl fills the cubicle. And then I feel wet washing past my toes, and looking down see water rushing from behind the bowl and flooding across the marble. "Oh," I say.

Grigor's Spanish sandals step backward and I hear wet splotching across the floor. "I'll get Security," he says, and the door opens and wheezes closed.

Pressing the button again, I watch more water flood across the floor. "Call Emergency Services too!" I shout, hoping he hears. Cistern half full and I press it again.

I bought a *Men of Emergency Services* calendar last week and a lot of those guys look definitely single.

Morgana Malone and the Case of the Blushing Bride

Tuesday, 25th February 2014

"Oh, God!" Seventeen eyes dart in Zebadie's direction. Looking at me as she lowers her head on the reception desk in exasperation, she breathes out and says, "I soooooo miss porn."

I look over the beige laminate counter into the waiting area. Mr Rubinstein, he of eye no. 17 and an eye patch, bobs up in his chair. I smile and nod, like it's every day the receptionist in a therapy practice admits to working as an adult entertainer in the so-recent past.

"Something caught in her throat," I say, as Mr Rubinstein's eyebrows and eye patch lower. "A bit of déjà vu, I think."

Zebadie – whose neon-blonde like-nylon hair is in thrown-together pigtails today – peers up at me, eyes glistening. "You know what kept me doing porn?" she says. "It wasn't the sex or the practical jokes or the catering, Morgana." And she sniffles at the thought. "It was the conversation. There was always a lot of great conversations happening on the set." A tear appears in the corner of her eye. (Just one.) She sighs, sits up, and reaching under the counter, pulls out a scrapbook with *Wedding Plans* sprayed in Bedazzled jewels on the cover. She opens it and the plastic gems smack the desktop. "That's what first attracted me to Grigor," she says, "his level of conversation. That" – she licks her finger and rifles through to the next page – "and his Porsche."

(It's only my second day here and already I have my favourite patients. "I luff your racink schtripe," Mr Rubinstein said to me earlier, when he walked in, nodding at the grey-brown regrowth yawning through the orange on my head. "They make you go fasta." Smiling under his eyepatch, his toupée undulated on his head like a motley possum caught in the air conditioning draught.)

"The only real downsides to a life in porn are laxatives and plastic surgery," Zebadie says. "And no paid holidays. But it's the kind of job that travels and no one judges you by how fake your orgasms sound because they're all fake. So it's kind of like a level playing field. You store up the real orgasms for the real players. I mean, you have to draw the line *somewhere*."

Zebadie flicks through her wedding planner. She's not really looking at the pages, but sits mesmerized by the colour and movement as each page flicks past at breakneck speed, her wrists working up and down and showing no sign of tiring.

"So I guess porn is paying for your trousseau," I say.

"Well, for my first marriage, it did." And then she touches my forearm with her hand, all blue-eyed wonder. "Don't tell Grigor, though," she whispers. "He still thinks he's the first one."

I look at the push-up bra holding her three and a half boob jobs and the coffee dripolator tan and the scorched hair –

"After my re-birthing," she cuts in, her voice grave and knowing, "of course. Re-birthing means you're also a virgin again." She covers her mouth with her hand, and burps. "Although I want to know if I can get my money back on that one: every morning when I wake up the first thing I smell is placenta. And I don't care what anyone says: that's just not normal."

A door opens and out steps Barry, Grigor's brother and partner in this psychiatry practice, and of course, my ex-brother-in-law. His hand under her elbow, Barry ushers out an older woman dressed in a black boiler suit, a red pillbox hat perched on her curly grey bob. "Susan will help you with your next appointment," he says.

Boiler suit looks at him, eyebrows quizzical.

"I mean Morgana," Barry says. "Sorry, *Morgana* will help you. *Morgana* will help you with your next appointment."

Sometimes I forget my real name is – was – Susan. And sometimes I forget Barry still calls me the name he first knew me by, when I first met him, when Grigor and I were first married.

Right hand on the mouse as the cursor rolls across the computer screen, I – the new office junior, though I *am* "up-managing" as Grigor told me – focus on looking important: back straight, jaw set, eyes steady.

"Tuesday the 4th at 11:00am," I ask, my eyes on the screen. Though it's not really a question. I type in her name, my hands clunky on the keyboard: *clunk clunk clunk.*

"Tuesday the 4th at 11:00am," Zebadie the office senior (she who's being "up-managed") repeats, large appointment book now open on the desk, her hand curving across the page as she carves the paper with her curly-curly cursive: *scr-a-tch ... scr-a-tch ... scr-a-tch.*

I click an icon on the screen and a printer spews out a green appointment slip. Reaching across, I tear it off the printer and hand it to boiler suit lady, who slips it inside her boiler suit breast pocket.

I don't know if Tuesday the 4th at 11:00am is good or bad. That's not what I'm paid to do, Grigor tells me, I'm here to work the new computer system and keep Zebadie on track and attend therapy sessions with Grigor when he thinks I need them, so there's some semi-déjà vu for me too.

Boiler suit lady is not even out through the door before Zebadie says, a little too loud, "Didn't you fuck him in the backseat of his Porsche?"

"Who?" I ask. "Which Porsche?"

"Barry."

"Well," I say, my voice low and directed towards the counter top, "it was Grigor's Porsche. But I *thought* it was Barry."

Zebadie's eyes bulge. "But they're not even identical."

"I know. But Grigor and I ... it was a very messy evening and I had a cold and I couldn't smell."

Zebadie shakes her head and smirks, like she's just discovered the Theory of Relativity while I can't even count to ten. She slaps the large appointment book shut, pushes it aside, then reaches for her wedding planner again. It opens on three long fabric swatches, pale purple ribbons stuck to the page with clear sticky tape.

"Lilac, mauve or lavender," Zebadie says. "It's so hard choosing the right colour for my bridesmaids." She pushes the scrapbook in front of me. "What do you think?"

I look at the fabric swatches again, shiny and pale purple and I can't decide which is lilac and which is mauve and which is lavender. I set my face in an interested look: eyebrows raised and eyes wide. "Choose the one that's easiest to spell."

Looking up, I see Grigor poking his head around the door. "Morgana?"

He cups his hand over the receiver but his voice draws me in – tones so even and measured and demanding to be listened to – so I hear every syllable like I'm sitting on his lap.

"I want it perfect for the wedding," he says. "My fiancée is giving it to me for a wedding gift. I want to remove this flaring" – he brushes his nostrils with his free hand – "and I want a more aquiline line. This bump" – now he touches just below the bridge of his nose – "is ruining an otherwise perfect profile."

Actually sitting on the black leather armchair – titanium frame, tight across the seat: "elegant but unyielding", as some catalogue would probably describe it – I cross my knees and my right ankle starts twitching like a metronome. I read the nameplate on the desk: Grigor Smiroveich™. When we married he was Grigor

Smith. Before that he was Greg Smith. Now he's a trademarked Russian.

He drops the receiver back into its cradle and opens the file marked *Morgana Malone* on his desk.

"You know what would be the perfect wedding gift," he says, closing my file again. And as he looks up, his eyes mist over. "Oh, I don't know if I dare."

He looks at his hands on the desk, strokes his nose again, and opens his mouth to speak. Then stops. Is he blushing?

"Your face is red, Grigor."

Grigor coughs. "It's just a bit of pre-surgery swelling," he says. "Marrying a former adult entertainer drives my need to improve my looks."

He opens my file again then snaps it shut.

"You know what would be the perfect wedding gift?" he says again, now looking straight at me.

A penis extension? I want to say.

"Something that will mean just as much to Zebadie as it will to me."

A penis extension? I want to say.

"We'd really like you to be Zebadie's matron of honour on our wedding day."

I think that's the day I'm having my penis extension, I want to say.

"Barry's going to be best man," he adds.

My jaw flaps in mid-air but nothing comes out of my mouth. So it's lucky the 'phone rings and Grigor picks it up.

Zebadie's telephone voice, shrill and nasal and garbled, pierces through the plastic.

"Yes," he says, "she's smiling and looking very pleased." And then he looks over at me. "Lavender, mauve or lilac?" Grigor asks. "Zebadie wants to know."

"Lavender," I say, presuming it's the right answer. But when I picture myself standing at the altar and taking Zebadie's bouquet of wild cherries and spinifex from her re-virginated hand, I can only see myself in pale violet.

Morgana Malone and the Mystery of the Opium Den

Tuesday, 25th March 2014

Mary Agnes flicks crust from the edge of her mouth with her finger and sits back into the armchair. Tucking in her triple chin, she looks at me and says, "Doesn't she, Morgana?"

In the mirror, I see tears welling in Zebadie's eyes.

(Zebadie's ex-co-star Virginella Vox pulled out last week, due to a Botox overdose, so I'm the lone bridesmaid now.)

Zebadie, blonde nest piled on her head, stands in front of the three-way mirror looking at her own reflection. Poured into a sateen wedding gown that's somehow off-the-shoulder *and* plunging to her navel, it also has a giant hood that I think, in its more gymnastic moments, might double as a train.

A tear rolls down Zebadie's cheek. She turns to look at Mary Agnes, her little teeth flashing, and Mary Agnes looks at me so Zebadie looks at me and then looks back at Mary Agnes. I don't know who to look at, so I stare in the mirror, at the widening grey-and-brown strip showing through my dyed-orange hair.

"Like I said," and fingers drumming on the worn velvet armrest Mary Agnes repeats her pronouncement: "You look like a whore."

I catch Zebadie's eyes again in the mirror. Her shoulders sag, and she looks like a helpless bunny – Playboy bunny; rabbit-caught-in-the-headlights bunny; victim of someone's cruel joke bunny – so I pipe up: "You mean professionally or do you mean personally?"

"All I said is," Zebadie whispers, the fabric flowers she holds in her hand – the *test bouquet* as the bridal shop assistant told us – jiggling as she shakes, "my right side is better so when we're standing at the altar thing I want to have my right side closer to the cameras and the audience."

There's no denying it, with her three and a half boob jobs, Zebadie's right side certainly creates a larger impression.

Mary Agnes raises an eyebrow.

"This is *my* wedding, Mum, may I remind you," Zebadie says.

Mary Agnes pulls herself up in her seat. Her chins wobble in time with the flowers shaking in Zebadie's hands. "I didn't come here to be insulted, Melissa," – Melissa is Zebadie's real name – "especially when I'm doing you a favour." Mary Agnes slumps back into the chair. "I don't care which side anyone sees as long as it's covered up!"

Zebadie throws the test bouquet on the floor at her mother's feet. The flowers lie squashed and faded, but actually, look quasi-tasteful against Mary Agnes's red

64

diamante-studded wedgies with velvet bows across the toes.

"I should have gone bowling instead," Mary Agnes continues, now waving her flabby arms and jabbing the air with her index finger, like a rapper. "It's the inter-zonal finals for the late Tuesday afternoon Mini-League. But no, you're getting married – again. So I'm helping you choose a wedding dress – again. Looking at you dressed like a slut – again again again!"

I cross my knees and put a finger on my lips, wetting the tip with my tongue. With wobbling chins and heaving bosoms and snapping nerves I can't help but think of Grigor's new nose job and what if Grigor has the same good side as Zebadie? Will they both want their right side to the camera? How will he kiss the bride? When I married Grigor thirteen years ago we had the ceremony in my mother's garden and he kissed me on the mouth afterwards and no one cared about profiles but if they both have the same best side, what will he do after the 'You may now kiss the bride' speech? Kiss her on the back of her head?

And then – I don't know why I say this, but it just flies out of my mouth: "Define *whore*?"

Like I'm the arbiter of all things whorish.

"If you'd loaned me the money I would have been able to get the left one done at the same time, Mum," Zebadie continues, like I'm not in the room. She's sniffing now, four layers of false eyelashes glistening in the yellow bride-to-be light.

I put my hand over my mouth and swallow a yawn.

"And it would have been a tax deduction so I would have paid you back when I got my tax return!" Zebadie says. "So it would have been a win-win-win situation all

65

round," and she points to her mother and then to herself and then to her own left breast.

Reflected in the mirrors, a door opens and a woman of about thirty – tall, long brown hair slicked down and pulled together at the nape of her neck – steps into the bridal sanctum. "Ho-ow's it going?" she asks as our heads snap to watch her. And before there's time for any reply, she looks snivelling Zebadie up and down and says, "Oo-oh! You look gor-orgeous!" The muscles in her face shift upward and her mouth curves into a smile and her voice bounces around the room, but the way her words stretch out isn't convincing: her eyes are wide but their light is extinct.

"You look tired," I say to her in the reflection. She pulls some of the dress fabric away from Zebadie's thigh and, shoulders slumping as she cranes to look, lets it fall. She must have done this thousands of times, I think, to make it look so ... spontaneous.

As she pulls more of the dress fabric away from Zebadie's thigh, like she's prepping Zebadie for a fashion shoot or a cakestand, I see her name badge. *Kylie Jay's World of Dream Weddings*, it says, in sparkly silver, and below that, *Hi, I'm Conradine.* But the sparkly silver is scratched, like it was caught on the bottom of her shoe as she walked across cement.

Conradine folds her arms under her breasts, and looks Zebadie up and down again, this time like she's a mannequin in a ... I don't know, a porn bridal shoot.

Zebadie turns to look in the mirror. She flicks out the bottom – or the crown – of the draping hood, and looks at her own bottom in the reflection.

"It's exci-i-ting, isn't it?" Conradine says, watching Zebadie in the mirror looking at her bottom. And as we watch her, Conradine unfolds her arms, laces her fingers together, locks her elbows, and stretching her palms outward, cracks her knuckles. "Ste-epping off into the re-est of your li-ife."

"Stepping in front of a runaway train!" says Mary Agnes.

"Grigor owns a Porsche, Mum!" Zebadie snaps. Like she's saying, *Grigor's developed the patent for world peace, Mum*. Or, *Grigor really loves me for the person I am inside*.

"Hmmm," says Mary Agnes, and shifts her flobbing arms on the worn velvet. We wait for the rest of her retort, but her lips are pursed.

"So, do you thi-ink you'll take it?" Conradine pipes up. "Because it looks one hu-undred percent stu-unning on you, you have ju-u-ust the fi-igure for it."

I watch Conradine's jaw extend and snap to get around those vowels. Maybe talking like that stops her from growing completely bored.

Zebadie shakes her head, and looks downcast at the hem gracing the floor. "I was really looking for something more 50's," she sniffs, the fussy customer again. "A bit more velour. A bit more glam. A bit more shinier. And I don't like the hood."

"We can always take the hood off," says Conradine.

"No, I want it bigger," Zebadie says.

"Were hoods that big in the 50's?" I ask. (I don't know why I do this, the conversation draws me in and words fly out of my mouth.) Now all eyes are on me. "I mean, big as in popular."

"Oh ye-es," says Conradine. "It was the e-e-era of the hood. The hood was derigeu-eu-eur in the 50's. It was only later that pe-eople stopped wea-earing them. When I think hoo-oods I always think 50's. Hoo-oods. Fi-if-ties.

Fi-if-ties. Hoo-oods. Hoo-oods. Fi-if-ties. Fi-if-ties. Hoo-oods."

I take it back. I don't think she's staving off boredom with her elongated vowels and snapping jaw. I think she's on laudunum.

The sun blazes deep in the western sky and we're standing by the kerb waiting for Grigor to screech up in his Porsche and drive us all to dinner at a new seafood restaurant right on the wharf at Port Adelaide called *Scabs*. ("I've cancelled all my patients," he told us, as he helped us into a taxi earlier this afternoon. "I can't solve people's deep psychological problems *and* escort them to and from the reception desk at the same time.")

Conradine stands around the corner, foot flat against the brick wall behind her, smoking a cigarette. Her shoulders are relaxed and her eyes are steady. Maybe it's just serving customers inside *Kylie Jay's World of Dream Weddings* that makes her sound like she works inside a centrifuge.

I turn to look at the rush hour traffic. I don't know how we'll all fit in Grigor's Porsche. I remember from the time I mistakenly fucked Grigor inside it, there's not a lot of room in the back seat of a Porsche. The jaws of life would have a hard time extracting anyone from that thing.

Though if Grigor skids into the *Scabs* car park and the Porsche spins off the wharf and we all crash into the water, I plan to grab on to Zebadie's right airbag and not let go. That should keep me afloat 'til the Water Rescue Squad arrives.

Morgana Malone and the Miracle of St. Francis Xavier

Friday, 25th April 2014

"Save me!" I say, as I duck between their legs. Crouching behind them, I look down at my toes poking through the lavender or mauve or lilac strappy bridesmaid sandals and hold my breath as their chanting continues.

One – two – three – four –

I look up, and I see their signs for the first time: 'Hubbard's Hoes' and 'Dianetics Disaster' and 'L. Ron is a shit!'

And hear them chant, "L. Ron Hubbard is weak! Chuck him in the creek!"

And through their legs I see the opposing forces, lolling behind a wooden stand, young women with ponytails and young men with skinny arms, and books and leaflets and smiles piled high. 'FEEL HAPPIER AND MUCH MORE CONFIDENT' – their banner declares – 'the Scientology Way' – their banner whispers.

What I thought I might find when I slammed the St. Francis Xavier Cathedral door on the wedding rehearsal was the remnants of the parade, men and women from the army and the navy and the air force marching past, their faces solemn as the crowd waved and the music intoned and the sun hid behind a cloud. It is, after all, Anzac Day, the public holiday where we commemorate the Australian and New Zealand Army Corps landing at Gallipoli in 1915 and their horrific loss. And well, Anzac Day is equally famous for its rainfall.

But the marchers have disappeared and the onlookers too and so there's just the Scientologists and the anti-Scientologists and me here in the middle of Victoria Square.

Five – six – seven – eight –

In the distance I hear Grigor's steps thundering towards me and Zebadie's shrill top note – "Come back, ya cunt!" – so I drop my bottom closer to the footpath and hunker down.

When Grigor asked me into his office yesterday afternoon I had no idea he would sink to his knees, wrap his arms around my legs and say, "I'm marrying the wrong woman on Saturday. You're the woman I love."

Why is it always the ex-wife-bridesmaid who's the last to hear about it?

"Does Zebadie know?" I asked.

(But I didn't know what else to say! It was an unusually warm day yesterday and the dress I was wearing was soft and filmy and with his head pressed against my crotch, I could already feel the dampness spreading. And there was this *ache* ...)

"No," he said, looking up at me. A breeze blew through the open window but not a hair on his head moved, it was lacquered so stiff. "But I thought I'd tell her the church had changed at the last minute. You know Zebadie's haphazard skills with the GPS." And he blinked.

I shake my head at the thought.

Nine – ten – eleven – twelve –

"Where's the fucking dog?!" Zebadie screams, a little closer this time, out of breath and stiletto heels snipping on the cement.

Zebadie had wanted a dog in the wedding, a schnoodle – part schnauzer, part poodle – and I was holding its diamante lead when, wedding rehearsal half over, Grigor turned to me, eyes wet and voice throbbing, and said, "I can't do this." And then my head began to spin and I think I smelled almonds and I thought, *No, no, no, I can't do this either* and as Grigor stepped towards me with his hand stretched out, palm up, eyes deep and imploring, I dropped my test bouquet and Zebadie's test bouquet and the dog lead slipped out of my hand and I sort of fell against a pew and then I turned around and wobbled up the aisle and, door slamming behind me, ran onto Wakefield Street.

I guess this probably means I needn't turn up for my admin job at Grigor's psychiatry practice on Monday either.

"Where is she?!" I hear Grigor's voice, dark and desperate. "What does she think she's doing?!"

It's then I hear the chanting has stopped and six faces are peering down at me. I know I must look a sight, and I touch the paper doily practice bridesmaid's cap pinned to my head, hiding much of the brown and grey regrowth yawning through the dyed orange.

"I'm just having a bad day," I say. "Please carry on."

But then the legs part and I see Grigor – and Zebadie standing behind him – glaring down at me. His eyes are black and thunderous and his nose looks extra pointy and I can't help but see the hair quivering in his now cavernous nostrils.

Thirteen – fourteen – fifteen – sixteen –

"You've lost your chance at being my matron of honour now!" Zebadie spits.

And Grigor, chest heaving and dribble on his chin, has the last word: "I hope you don't regret this, Morgana."

Morgana Malone and the Riddle of the Sands of Time

Sunday, 25th May 2014

The sand thwumps out of the upturned jar. Well, it would, except it's not sand.

"This is not sand," Ludmilla says, looking down at the coloured crystals spreading across the table. Her dull brown hair streaked with grey frames her face in a lank way that says, *I don't know what else to do with it and who cares anyway?!*

I pat my own hair – blown-about orange bob with ever-widening grey-brown re-growth striped across the top – and look down at the table too. The table that ... I don't know ... but when I read her small ad in the *Psychic News* I thought would be flat and probably smooth, perhaps metal or at least Laminex but not this pitted old wooden thing with dips and knots and channels in the grain.

I place the jar down on the table with a glassy clink. The pink straw resting beside it rolls toward me and settles in a crack.

"Well, no," I say, digging the straw out with my finger. "But I *did* get it *near* the beach. And *I* bought it, it wasn't someone else who bought it, it was me, with my money. I picked it up off the shelf and, you know ..." I would keep talking but I think my voice has floated off down the street and across the Southern Ocean.

I pick the straw up.

Ludmilla sits back in her chair, shoulders wheezing against the vinyl. As she opens her mouth I see her teeth are a dull beige.

"But I am a sand reader," she says, crossing her arms under her cavernous cleavage so her breasts spill over her pale forearms. "I need the sand to be reading your fortune and this is just ..." – her cheeks fill with air and she exhales, her breath slow and small across the table but direct against my face, and I smell garlic and onion and what could be borscht: maybe that's her power, really, windpower, not this sand reading stuff – "... it is not the correct sand."

Well, yes, no, I agree, it's not sand. It's a jar of bath salts really, originally bought with the dark colours layered at the bottom – grape and purple and lilac – then up to the pinks – shocking and coral and flamingo – and then baby pink and cream and white ... but then I unscrewed the top and spooned out the first two layers and shook it up like a martini, shaking and shaking and shaking and then I stirred the first two layers back in with the same spoon.

(I was given those bath salts in a Secret Santa three Christmases ago.)

(And that shaking was the most exercise I had all day.)

I put the straw back on the table.

(Walking out the front door has been an exercise in discipline I currently don't have much of. It's safer to sit inside in the dark. And I have a lot of time now since I stopped working as the admin junior at Grigor's psychiatry practice, up-managing Zebadie the porn star / receptionist. So I just sit in the dark and think. And thinking is a good way to *not* spend money when you don't have a job.)

"But it is all *focked*," Ludmilla says, breasts bobbing in indignation on her forearms. "I am supposed to be giving you a straw and we both put on some glasses for protecting our eyes and then you blow on the sand and make some pretty pictures and I interpret them for your future but –" and she throws her hands in the air so her breasts thwop back against her stomach "– this is some pretty pictures in a bottle and is not some sand you get from your favourite spot on the beach that has some meanings in your life." She crosses her arms again – this time, *over* her breasts – and pushing out her bottom lip, she breathes out, her straggly grey-brown fringe fluttering against her forehead. Which I now see has a large red pimple with a bulbous yellow head glistening in the middle of it.

"They were in a jar," I say, eyes popping, grasping for the truth amongst this psychic mess, "it's a *jar*, Ludmilla, it's not *focked*. A jar." And I stab a free spot on the table with my index finger. "A *jar* is not a *bottle*. And a jar is not *focked* by definition because it's a *jar*. A *bottle* is *tapered*" – my hands flash through the air outlining a tapering bottle – "and has a small *opening* at the *top* but a *jar* is the

75

same circumference all the way up, usually." And again, my hands carve the air creating an impromptu jar. "Like a wheat *silo* except made of *glass* and a lot *smaller*."

I don't know why I'm *emphasising* certain *words*.

I sit back against the chair and my shoulders whisper against the vinyl.

Actually, I don't know why I'm doing anything.

"Can't you interpret bath salts?" I ask, my voice thin and wan and nothing. "I can blow on the bath salts with the straw and make *prettier* pictures."

Ludmilla leans forward and, breasts now resting on the table, sinks her chin into her hand.

"But my talent is reading the sand that has some special reason for you," Ludmilla says, "and since you telephoned me and saying my ex-husband is giving me the sack and now I have no job and my life is in the toilets and I need some hope."

I look down at the sand, I mean the bath salts, and they're all mixed into a murky pinky sugary brown so, if you were drunk enough, you could spoon them into your mouth then pretend you were having a diabetic episode.

"But if you cannot make a trip to the beach with a bucket and a ... a ... you know, a *dig dig* thing then ... to save your life and to get some directions then your life is *focked* and I cannot help you if you cannot help yourself."

It comes from somewhere, I don't know where, but a smile appears at the corner of my mouth. "Oh, you mean *fucked*?" I say. But the way I say it, I say 'fecked'. Like Ludmilla would say if she were imitating my Australian accent.

"Focked, fecked, fooked," she chants, "whenever, it is all the same for you."

"Yes," I say. And picking up the straw, I put it to my lips and blow hard, covering Ludmilla's vast continental shelf with my focked future.

Morgana Malone and the Miracle of Christmas

Wednesday, 25th June 2014

"Be holding this," Ludmilla says, and pushes a samovar into my arms.

The samovar is big and silver and crushes against my breastbone because it weighs a ton. (Or tonne, if you want to be metric about it. Or actually, 1.016 tons, if you want to be *accurate* and metric although it could be the other way around. Not that I adore the Imperial measurement system but since I lost my job at Grigor's therapy practice and don't have a lot of money and spend a lot of time alone at home, I'm on the internet quite often. And I found a website just the other day comparing metric to Imperial and it was *mesmerising*.)

Meanwhile, Ludmilla is busy piling things up on the kitchen bench. What looks like a pasta press. Then what she said is an exotic blini maker. (She didn't say *exotic*, I did, or thought it when she lugged it inside – 'gee, that looks exotic,' I thought – and she saw me looking at it and said, "No peeking – it makes blinis.") Then her famous borscht pot. And then another pot she's using to make 'sochivo' (aka 'kutia', just depends upon which part of Russia you come from. Although I think Ludmilla is not from Russia but is an ethnic Russian from the Ukraine or maybe even Georgia, it's hard to work out just where she's from because when she's talking about her childhood she gets excited and spits a lot.)

Thinking of Ludmilla spitting makes me think of sweet Mr Rubinstein, who would come in every day for therapy. Or as he'd say, "because I am enjoying some chillink here in the waiting room." Mr Rubinstein of the eye patch and the toupée, who loved the widening grey-brown strip on my head. (I am growing out the orange I had it dyed because (1) I really don't like looking like a carrot and (2) I can't afford to get it dyed orange again by a professional hairdresser.)

My mind whips back to 'sochivo' or 'kutia', the special dish of boiled wheat sweetened with honey and sometimes dried fruit, which I know about because I looked it up on the internet. Ludmilla emailed me the links. She said it would be a nice gesture of international goodwill if I made it for the dinner party tonight, especially because I'm not Russian. "And I know you are not Russian," she said, "because no Russians are having orange hair."

(But I've never been that good at boiling wheat! So I'm going to pay her to boil the wheat instead. Or, give her a big discount on her first month's rent. Apparently making 'sochivo' can take hours.)

"What is your matter?" Ludmilla glares at me. "Your eyes are spinning spinning spinning inside your head and your brain is looking like it is cooking."

The samovar, I realise, with its cute green filigreed frog bobbling on the very top, almost touching my nostrils, is crushing the life out of me but there is no free space on any of the kitchen benches or the table to put it down and it's too magnificent and ornate and curlicued (and heavy and awkward) to put it down on the floor so I lean against the wall still clutching it but actually, it's the pantry door I'm leaning against and then I realise almost immediately as Ludmilla makes a beeline for me that I'm in her way.

"You are standing where I need to going," Ludmilla says. "Salt, salt, I need salt!"

I sort of lob out of her way – or shuffle, really, with the samovar in my arms – and then I realise I don't have any salt anyway. Because I never have salt.

"I don't have any salt, Ludmilla," I say, as she pulls the pantry door open and the 15-month calendar – January 2013 to March 2014 – smacks against the back of the door. "Remember last week when you were here, you had to use sugar because I didn't have any salt?"

Ludmilla stops in her tracks. "No salt?! You have ... no ... salt?!"

"No," I say, "I don't really cook with salt."

"No salt?!"

"No," I repeat. "No salt." Although, really, I'm not cooking with anything at the moment because I'm not really cooking because I'm not really eating.

Ludmilla closes the pantry door. "Then lucky lucky lucky you for I am moving in with you," she says. "So I know now why you be so skinny." And she stretches it out, *skee-ee-nee*, like I'm suddenly a lot taller too.

Although, if anything, if you looked at me – *really* looked at me – you'd say I was shorter.

"Where can I put this samovar, Ludmilla? It's pulling my arms out of their sockets."

"And lucky lucky lucky you our first meal together is for Christmas in July in June," she says. She steps over to the sink and looks through the window at the grey early winter sky. "No rain," she adds. "There is winter but there is no rain."

"Could you clear a spot on the bench?" I say, waddling over to the sink. This samovar is really killing me but if I drop it, it's going to dent the floor. Which is concrete but probably the dentable kind.

"But Christmas in July in June with *no salt*?" she says, turning to scowl at me, her mouth a frown and a smile at the same time, so really, just skewed. "Im – pos – si – ble!" she says, like she's just discovered the word and she's trying it out. "Impossible, impossible." She picks up her battered blue vinyl handbag from its perch on top of the exotic blini maker and slings it into the crook of her elbow. "*No* salt, *no* Christmas in July in June. So we buy salt."

The samovar rattles on the back seat as I drive Ludmilla in my faded watermelon pink Nissan Micra to the nearest supermarket. Ludmilla's first gesture as my new house-mate is this Christmas in July party except it's not July yet, it's June, but it *is* the 25th. Accepting this party is my first housematerly act of diplomacy.

("Then we can be celebrating the big Australian tradition, Christmas in July," Ludmilla had said, when she told me it would be a good idea if I got a housemate. Like her. And soon. Like next week (which is actually this week now). When she came to my house to give me a free salt reading. At her own instigation. Except, of course, I didn't have any salt.

"But we don't do Christmas in July here," I'd said, licking the rolling pin before running it across the sugar I'd spread across the kitchen table. "Some of us barely do Christmas in December. We're just going through the motions 'til we can go to the beach for the summer holidays."

Taking the rolling pin from my grasp, she'd glanced at the sugar impressions made on the wood, then looked me up and down, raised an eyebrow, and harrumphed.

"And it won't even be July next week," I'd added, "it'll still be June."

"Christmas in July *in June*," she'd said. "I bring my samovar and we celebrate *big* Australian Christmas in July in June tradition.")

Ludmilla opens the passenger door and slings the 10-kilo bag of salt on the floor in front of the seat. Then, "What is this?" she says, and picks up the white envelope she was sitting on as we drove to the supermarket.

She holds it closer to read it, her thin lips mouthing my name on the front.

"It's from Grigor," I say. "That's his writing."

"Ach, but he writes not like a Russian," Ludmilla says.

"He's not Russian," I say. "His real last name is Smith."

"He writes not like a Russian," she repeats.

"Yes, his real last name is Smith," I say again. And then, before we go another round of *he writes not like a*

Russian / his real last name is Smith, "I've been meaning to open it all week," I say. "It's just been lying there on the seat. I came out one morning and found it stuck to the windscreen."

Doors slam and I turn the key in the ignition. Just as I steer the faded Nissan Micra right, out of the car park, I hear ripping paper and turn to catch Ludmilla opening the letter.

"*As you have ruined my life and made a mockery of my wedding,*" she reads. (Then to me but more to herself, "Who is this *mockery*?" she snorts.) "*Here is the bill for my ruination.*" And then to herself but more to me, "There is a lot of serious numbers."

The samovar skids across the backseat as I pull over to the kerb, and right foot on the brake and with the engine still running, take the letter from her hand. My eyes run down the accompanying page of numbers. It's an itemised account of everything spent (and not paid for, by the look of things) for his wedding. The schnoodle, the platinum wedding rings, Grigor's rhino-platsy, the vegan wedding bouquets ... oh, everything.

So did Grigor marry Zebadie or was *that* passed on to someone else too?

"But this is *verrry* Russian thing," Ludmilla pronounces, her chin nodding. "What is *yacht*?" she says, but she says it like it's spelled, 'y-a-ch-t'.

I shake my head. Can he come after me for the money?

Ludmilla rips the letter from my hand. "Look," she points at the bill, "you know bad people, bad people be advantaged over you. So get rid of bad people."

I pull on the handbrake, turn the key and the engine shudders to a stop.

"Christmas in July in June is here," Ludmilla says. "Maybe you meet a nice *real* Russian man."

I look out the driver's window. It's not raining but everything is a watery blur.

"Okay, your friend Ludmilla, I help you. I cook you 'sochivo'," she adds, "for free. Okay?"

I turn to see her peering at me. And, smiling so her beige teeth show past her thin lips, she pats my knee.

I twist and look at the backseat, at the silver samovar resting between two seatbelt buckles. And wonder who should I smash over the head with it first: Grigor, or Ludmilla?

Morgana Malone and the Mystery of the Manna from Heaven

Friday 25th July 2014

"Morgana Malone?"

I turn and see a young man, high cheekbones on a thin face and short dark hair atop deep brown eyes. He's looking at me through the open driver's window of a shiny, dark blue car. It's cold and the sky above is that depressing pale grey we all grow to know and loathe over the Australian winter. No rain, just cold and grey and dull dull dull. But it's a quiet suburban neighbourhood and we appear to be the only two people around – me on the footpath and he in his car with the engine still running in the middle of the street.

I stuff the leaflets back into my cotton hold-all – it's too cold to do two things at once – while I talk to this charming man. I want to know how he knows me.

"Morgana?" he asks, his eyebrows aquiver. And he smiles. "You must be, it's your hair, it's so ... *orange.*"

I brush my hair with my hand, which is past my shoulders now, but it unsettles the beanie on top of my head – I hate beanies but it's keeping my head warm – and the hat falls to the ground. So I bend down, and the cowl neck of the thick jumper looped across my chest swoops down in front as I pick the beanie up off the footpath.

He lets out a large whistle. "Whoa! It *is* you, that racing stripe is so sexy!"

I stand up and do the usual cramming of the beanie on my head, pulling it down over the grey-brown regrowth. I want to have my hair dyed again by a professional hairdresser – as opposed to an amateur – but it's taking a while to earn the money. And I've had a lot of bad luck job-wise (and bad luck life-wise) since I stopped working as junior admin officer at Grigor's therapy practice way back in ... oh, April ... and then Ludmilla moved out and moved in with her kitchenhand cousin Sergei and then –

"No, don't cover it up," he says, "that stripe is hot! Opi was right, you are one sexy mama." Leaning his elbow on the window frame, he grins. He has no gaps in his teeth.

When I stepped outside this morning to deliver more junk mail – my savings are running out and I don't have any other job and it gets me out in the fresh (cold, dull dull dull) air and I get a lot of knuckle exercise with all the folding beforehand plus I thought it would be a good way to meet single men – I had not expected the third degree (if this is the third degree, though, it could be the first, second or fourth degree instead) from a young man with short dark hair, deep brown eyes and all those teeth who also knows my name and who also might be single.

But I can't help it, it comes from nowhere. "I'm probably as old as your mother."

"Yeah?" He reaches forward and the engine stops idling. (He must want to talk to me, he's stopped dead in the middle of the street.) "How old would that be?" he says, and settles back into the seat.

"Forty-seven," I say. "Today, in fact. I'm forty-seven today."

"Yeah? Dang, me too! It's my birthday today as well. I'm twenty-three."

I pull the strap of my hold-all further on to my shoulder. "It's really your birthday today?"

"Nah, just kidding," he says, and grins again. This guy, he's a great grinner.

"Me too, I'm just kidding too," I say, though it actually *is* my birthday today, and I *am* forty-seven now. I'm just trying to forget. "Do you want me for something?"

"Are you busy?"

Am I busy? Well, I could be busy, I think, wondering what his plans are. If he's stalking me then yes, I'm definitely busy. But if he wants to get to know me and buy me a drink and whisk me away to somewhere that's sunny and warm and not dull dull dull grey, then no, I might not be so busy after all.

"Well, I'm stuffing letterboxes with advertising for *Knights of the Polish Cross* sauvignon blanc," I say, half-flashing him a tri-fold leaflet sticking out of my hold-all, "if that counts as *busy*." I step off the kerb and hold-all swinging against my hip, cross the three metres to the car.

"Opi is right – you are a *damn* fine woman, Morgana Malone."

I'm standing by the driver's door now, hands in the pockets of my corduroy trousers. "Who's Opi?"

"Opi. You know, Julius Rubinstein, from where you used to work." But he says it Germanically, *Yoo-lee-ess.* Yoo-lee-ess Roo-bin-shtine.

"Oh, Mr Rubinstein!" I smile, happy to remember my favourite patient at Grigor's therapy practice, and I rock back on my heels. "No one can carry off an eye patch and toupée quite the way he can. How is he?"

"Good," he says. "Okay," he says. "Well, not too good really," he says. "A bit fucked."

Mr Rubinstein is sitting up in bed, his toupée perched further back on his head so it looks like it's revving up for a take-off, and his eye patch removed, a darkened sewn-up hole where his eye once was. A nurse holds his wrist with one hand and with her watch in the other, checks his pulse. Which strikes me as old-fashioned (isn't there a robot to do this?) but then, with a toupée and eye patch and all, Mr Rubinstein is an old-fashioned kind of man.

"It is lovely to see you, my dahlink," he says, smiling against the pillows. "You and your lovely orange hair, just like my late, dear wife."

"And it's lovely to see you, too," I say, but it's not. A tube reaches in through his left nostril and a drip is attached to his right arm. And his skin is grey, near to translucent, and it's the middle of winter and a little chilly on the ward but sweat beads on his forehead, and his arms and the skin stretched across his collarbone are shiny with sweat. Even in the short time since I last saw him – an everyday sight until I left the job in late April – he's older and thinner and frailer and closer to the end.

I sniff and the room smells of sickly-sweet old man sweat but I smile at him anyway. I don't know whether to kiss his cheek or hold his other hand or what, so I just stand at the end of the bed. Which allows Seth – his grandson, the one who found me walking the streets delivering *Knights of the Polish Cross* junk mail – time to open the folder at the end of the bed and glance over his medical notes.

"My grandson is makink sure I have the best care in the hospital," Mr Rubinstein says. "He is a *brilliant* medical student and he will be a *brilliant* doctor. But seeink you is the best medicine, my dear, always the *best*."

I smile again. I'm smiling but I don't know what else to do. There's no reception desk separating us and now I'm just the visitor, not the person printing invoices and picking up the 'phone and doing all the things Zebadie didn't have the insight or interest to do. I'm just someone who was picked up on the street by a man half her age and whisked in for a visit.

The nurse returns Mr Rubinstein's hand to the mattress and taking the medical file from Seth's grasp, opens it on the tray table beside the bed and scribbles inside the folder.

"It's Morgana's birthday, Opi," Seth says, ignoring the nurse. And he winks at me.

"How old are you today, my dear? Not a day over twenty-two!"

"Forty-seven," I say. And to Seth I say, "Actually, it *is* my birthday."

"Yeah, I know," Seth adds. "It's *my* birthday too."

Mr Rubinstein yawns, his mouth full of big yellow teeth and a furry, white tongue.

"You need to drink more, Opi," Seth says. "Keep your fluids up."

The nurse wheels the tray table over Mr Rubinstein's legs, and taking a plastic cup filled with water and a straw from the bedside cabinet, plonks it down on the tray table.

"I just thought you might like a visitor, Opi," Seth says. And then to me, "Opi talks about you a lot."

"You need to keep your fluids up, Mr Rubinstein," the nurse says, patting his leg. Then she slots the medical notes back in their wire cage at the end of the bed and, white shoes squeaking on the lino, walks out of the room.

Mr Rubinstein opens his eyes wide and lifts up his arms, as if beholding something. "Such a vision," he says, I think to me.

"She was hard to track down," Seth says.

"You must come back and visit me when I am feelink better," Mr Rubinstein adds. And closes his eyes. Then he opens one, just a little. "Beauty always makes me feel better."

"Was I really that hard to track down?" I ask, as we walk out onto North Terrace to the beeping horns and gear changes of Friday mid-afternoon traffic. "Did you have to go to the police or scour the 'phone book or the electoral roll or dental records?"

I look at Seth side-on – high cheekbones on a thin face and short dark hair atop deep brown eyes. And am struck by how much he looks like Grigor. And he's a doctor too.

"No," says Seth, looking into my eyes and grinning again. "Wanna go back to my place for a birthday fuck?"

Morgana Malone and the Mystery of the Family Trust

Monday 25th August 2014

"Don't look at them!" Jane says, tucking them under her chair.

I lean sideways in my seat and peer at her feet.

"Don't look at them, I said! I don't even know if I can stock them." Jane opens her folder on the table – "papyrus," she notes, "imported from the Maldives," – and taking out a business card, hands it to me.

NOT made in China, I read.

décor • clothing • collectibles, I read underneath.

... for the incredibly discerning, I read under that.

Then, *127a King William Road.*

"It's a nightmare getting stock not made in China," Jane says, picking up her chai latte. "A nightmare!"

She puts her cup down on the table again with a clink, rattling the plates left over from lunch – black quinoa and juju bean salad for her (the Monday lunch special) and haloumi, lettuce and drizzled macadamia oil focaccia for me – then slides a foot across the tiles and into the open.

"They're made in Tibet," she says, "of bamboo and yak leather. But which Tibet? *Chinese* Tibet or *Tibet* Tibet?"

The brown strips across her feet are crinkly, but so too is her skin – nothing covering them but the yak strips and blue with winter cold.

"And isn't the Dalai Lama from *Indian* Tibet?!" she continues. "These are the decisions I'm faced with. You are lucky you don't have a career or a husband or children or a new business to set up."

I gaze around the café, and sip my double strawberry milkshake through a straw as sugary strawberry syrup wafts up from the glass. Pale sun streams through the window, a reminder that spring – has it really been that long? – is not far away. Almond trees have already blossomed and the apricot tree in the back garden of the house I rent is smothered with white flowers. (Ludmilla, my former housemate, visited only yesterday and eyed the blossom, dollar signs spinning in her head as she calculated how many buckets she would need to strip the free fruit from the lower branches in a few months.)

I pull my cardigan closer across my breasts.

"But we need to talk about Mum and the cake shop," Jane adds. "When was the last time you saw her?"

I shake my head. "I've sort of been keeping to myself lately."

Jane runs her fingers through her hair. Which is naturally auburn, not unlike the colour I thought my hair might turn out when I had it dyed orange.

"Mum can't keep the cake shop up much longer," she says. "She's seventy-two and on her own and she needs help."

(When we were growing up I always wanted hair like Jane's. Everyone loved it. *Jane has such gorgeous hair, so thick and auburn and shiny*, was a comment her hair always earned. I wanted hair like hers, so everyone would envy me.

Now of course, with my dye growing out and the grey-brown roots expanding across my head, I have hair people feel sorry for.)

Jane clears her throat then looks straight at me.

"And you don't have a career or a husband or children or a new business to set up or even a job so you'll have to be the one to take over the cake shop because I *do* have a career and a husband and children and a new business to set up." Jane breathes out. "*NOT made in China* won't set itself up, you know, and it's a business that I can well see will change the face of modern retailing."

I suck more double strawberry milkshake through the straw, my slurping noisy on the bottom of the glass. And then mention the unmentionable. "Why doesn't Mum sell the cake shop?"

Jane's mouth is a big 'O'. And then she gulps and collects her breath. "We'd never get what the cake shop is worth if we sold it in the current economic climate. And the cake shop is a family business. It'd be dreadful if it went out of the family. And let's face it Morgana, you stopped temping in January to work in your ex-husband's practice, and you left that *months* ago and *you're* not doing anything else so *you're* the obvious one to step in and help Mum." She purses her lips, and raises an eyebrow. "It's no different from when we were kids and we worked there on Saturday morning. She's seventy-two and on her own, and she needs help and it's time you stopped being so selfish and started thinking of others."

"But I'm seeing someone. We're talking about moving in together."

"And you know I've always had a head for business," Jane says, snapping the stud on her papyrus folder from the Maldives shut. "You know I know a lot about these things."

"So why don't *you* step in and work at the cake shop?" I suggest, assuming she's completely ignoring my news. "If anyone can keep it afloat, you can."

Jane sits back in her chair. "So who is this person you're seeing? Even though you're *sort of* keeping to yourself and don't have time to see your own mother."

Hmm, now I have to tell her.

"Well, you know," I say, "he has a bright future as a doctor and he's very good-looking and comes from a wealthy family and he's twenty-three."

"Twenty-three!" Jane says. "That's disgusting. You're old enough to be his mother." And a moment later, her eyes widen and raising an eyebrow again she looks directly at me and asks, "Is he good?"

A tall man with wavy brown hair and wearing a dark blue suit stands in the middle of the café and is looking at us.

"Is he good?" Jane asks again.

The tall man with wavy brown hair and wearing a dark blue suit is now two tables away.

"Are you just going to ignore me, Morgana?"

I snap my head to look at her because she never calls me Morgana and today she's called me that twice. I changed my name to Morgana a decade and a half ago and she's never –

"Susan?"

"Yes," we both say.

I look across the table at Jane. Who is now touching the ends of her naturally auburn hair.

The tall man with wavy brown hair and wearing a dark blue suit says, "You're both Susan?"

"No," we both say.

"Susan is my former name," I say, sounding very formal.

"And Susan is my new name," Jane tells him, and then looking at me across the table, she points at the business card she gave me and says, "for business purposes. It's on my card." And she flips over the card and there it is plain as day, *Susan Green-Baye*, her new name, which is actually my old name, with her husband's surname hyphened on the end.

"But *Susan Green* is my name."

"It *was* your name but it's not now, it's mine." And she smiles up at the tall man.

No one says anything. Perhaps the tall man's name is Susan Green too.

The tall man looks at me and then at Jane. "So which Susan used to be married to Grigor Smiroveich?" he asks.

"*She* did," the new Susan Green hyphen Baye says. "That was a looong time before I was ever Susan."

The tall man smiles. "Then this is for you," he says, and places a white envelope in front of me. "Have a nice day."

He hasn't cornered the next table over and I know what it is.

"What is it?" my sister (it's easier to call her that now) asks.

I pick the envelope up and without opening it, start ripping it into pieces. "Just Grigor still trying to get more money out of me for his cancelled wedding," I say.

"Don't look to me if you need money because I haven't got any," she says. "I have a husband and children and a business to support." She waves her hand in the air to signal a waitress.

I stare at the envelope and its contents, now a messy white paper pile on the table.

"It's all part of my business strategy," the new Susan continues. "Which I would not expect you to understand because you don't have a head for business like I do."

My eyes blur. She's expecting me to say something but I'm not going to say anything. What I want to do is shove the messy pile of paper down her throat and make her eat it.

"I went to a business specialist – she's very New-Agey – and she said *Jane* was not a good name for a businesswoman but *Susan* is."

The words are stuck in my throat. I breathe out and the paper flutters on the table. I can't look at my sister. So I look past her and out the window and I see Seth standing on the footpath: he with the bright future as a doctor who's very good-looking with high cheekbones on a thin face and short dark hair atop deep brown eyes and comes from a wealthy family and is twenty-three. I'd asked him to meet me after lunch. And my heart lurches inside my ribcage because, if ever I need rescuing, it's now.

"I had to take a bottle of sand from a place that's special to me but I didn't have any time to go to the beach so I just took a bucket and spade to the local kindergarten and got it from their sand pit. She's a sand reader."

I pick up my handbag from the spare chair beside me.

"And you weren't using your old name any more and it's a free country," she adds.

I stand up and look down at her. "I was hoping to start a new life again and I thought it might be nice to start by getting my old name back."

A waitress watches me as, high heels clacking on the floor, I head towards the door and a grinning Seth standing outside. I smile as I stop at the counter.

"Please send the lunch bill to this address," I say, handing the waitress the *NOT made in China* business card my sister gave me. "And mark it, *Attention: Susan*."

Morgana Malone and the Mystery of the Secret Gift

Thursday 25th September 2014

"La Petite Fleurette Select Patisserie and Gifterie," I say into the receiver.

"Is that the Royal Rose Cake Shop?" a voice, sing-song wavery, says on the end of the line. "I'm looking for the Royal Rose Cake Shop."

"Yes, we *were* the Royal Rose Cake Shop," I say, "we just have a new name. But it's the same service and we make the same cakes and we're at the same address."

"You haven't changed your range of cakes?" the older woman asks.

This happens two, three, seventeen times a day with Mum's old customers. And I curse Jane – my sister, who's still the new Susan (because I'm still the old Susan) – for changing the name of Mum's cake shop, hoping it will make the business more saleable when Mum decides to retire. Or when my sister decides it's time for Mum to retire.

I breathe in, and smell the sugary-sweetness of years of vanilla sponges and fruit cakes and cream puffs and lemon meringue pies and pavlovas.

"Oh good," the older woman sighs. "I always order a triple Victoria sponge for family birthdays and I need to order two. The family's getting so large now one triple Victoria sponge isn't enough."

I scribble *2 x triple Victoria sponges* and her name (which means nothing to me when she tells me but the way she says it, she obviously thinks it should) and her 'phone number on the order form – a newly-printed pad of them with the newly-minted *La Petite Fleurette Select Patisserie and Gifterie* at the top in pink curly-curly cursive – then tear if off the pad and place it in the *Orders – In* tray beside the 'phone. I want to ask her if, by *the family's getting so large*, she means in number or in size, but it's not always a good thing to ask a customer just how fat her family is, in case their weight *is* tipping the Richter scale.

"What's a *Gifterie*?" she says.

My face flushes and my armpits are suddenly sticky. I hate stammering the official "the *Gifterie* is an exclusive gift shop offering a select range of giftware." When instead I want to say *Hey, it's stocked with the stuff Jane / Susan ordered for her* NOT Made in China *shop that was accidentally made in China after all.*

So instead I say, "Thanks for your order," a little too loudly, and hang the 'phone back in its cradle.

And that's when I hear a voice, harsh enough to scratch glass on a rainy day. "I'm looking for Morgana Malone."

I step through the doorway, from the backroom into the main part of the shop, and sidle up to Mum behind the counter.

Mum's powdery face lights up, like she's forgotten I'm here. "There's someone to see you, love."

Mum's grey eyes are revealing ... well, not a lot, really. What they *are* saying, is that she knows nothing of this woman. Who I see has long dyed-brown hair pulled off a face with no makeup, pulled back under a small blue headscarf. And is wearing a white blouse. And a longish skirt with small blue flowers spread across it. I don't know what she's wearing on her feet because I can't see over the counter but given the top half of her outfit, probably flat white sandals.

"Morgana!" she says.

And then I piece the voice and the blue eyes and the growing-back eyebrows together and realise that underneath the new hair and the 50's housewifey fashion statement it's –

"Zebadie," I say, clasping my hands behind my back.

I am *so* glad I'm standing behind the counter. Otherwise she'd rush over and throw her arms around me, pressing me against those massive ... my God, no wonder I didn't recognise her! Her three and a half boob jobs are gone too! She's been gutted, filleted, her breastwork lipo-suctioned out of her and replaced by something new. Or maybe something old.

Standing against the spring sun shining through the shop window, she's almost ... concave.

And then I remember the last time we met – the day of the wedding rehearsal when I was supposed to be her bridesmaid – she called me a *cunt*.

And I can't help it, it's so obvious I have to say something. And hand at my cleavage, "What happened to your –"

"Oh those old things," and Zebadie waves her hand in the air, like they're yesterday's news. "I had them refashioned after I got the hostess job on the Plymouth Brethren Home Shopping Network."

I'm about to say, *So once again you've used your breasts for a career move,* but instead, Mum draws herself up to her full height, which is just above my shoulder, and says, "So you're the one who called my daughter a *cunt*?!"

Zebadie smiles. "Look, I'm not here to talk about how cunty or how *uncunty* your daughter was," she says, "trying to steal my fiancé from on top of me the day before my wedding. But what I *am* here to tell you is that" – and here she pierces me with those blue blue eyes and I wonder, just *what* is she going to say now, when she says – "Grigor forgives you."

I stand there.

Just looking.

I don't know what to say.

It's not that I'm waiting for someone else to butt in – which is normal when my family is around – but my lips are dry and my armpits are sticky and my mouth opens and nothing comes out.

"He wants you to know that. And he's dropping all the charges against you, too," Zebadie adds.

"What *charges*?" Mum asks, eyes fierce and her chin indignant.

"Breach of promise and criminal intent to bankrupt," Zebadie recites, like she's reading off a charge sheet.

Mum leans over the counter, which is not too difficult because she's 73 and stooping comes naturally. "My daughter was over *Grigor*" – and she spits his name out like it's a rancid olive – "years ago. She's seeing a lovely young man now who comes from a very good family and he has wonderful prospects." And she pats the counter, like she's scored a point on a quiz show.

For the second time in as many minutes my face flushes and now the crooks of my elbows are sticky. My 73-year old mother is defending my choice of boyfriend. Soon she'll be saying the 24-year age difference between Seth and me is something to be cherished.

"Grigor is turning over a new leaf," Zebadie says, "and he's moving on. He'll be on parole in six months."

"*Parole*?!" says Mum.

Zebadie tilts her head and for a second I expect something to fall out of her ear. "The one thing the Plymouth Brethren Home Shopping Network has taught me," she says, "is Christian forgiveness. And pretty soon Grigor will have his Porsche out of the pawn garage and things will be good again."

Ah, so that's it, I think, as Zebadie turns around and heads for the door. She still wants the Porsche.

"Let's hope that while you're waiting for the Porsche," Mum calls after her, "the Plymouth Brethren Home Shopping Network teaches you some manners."

Zebadie smoothes her blouse over her breasts. And her eyes pop, like she's still surprised at their lack of contours. "I'm just the Messenger," she says. "But this is from me." And she points at my hair, the top half grey and brown and the bottom half faded orange. "Get your hair dyed again Morgana because you look like a bad drag queen! Ya cunt!"

§

We're having a cup of tea. As in, "Let's have a nice cup of tea," so it's Mum and me sitting at the table in the backroom. Mum sips tea from a fine china cup saying "Nothing like a nice cuppa" and "Good riddance to bad rubbish" and "I don't think the Plymouth Brethren Home Shopping Network knows what it's in for" and "She doesn't have the right-shaped head for a scarf, does she?" and "She does have a point about your hair colour though."

And I just sip tea.

Tingaling. The front doorbell rings again.

Turning her wrist to look at her watch, "That'll be the postie," Mum says, and putting her cup down on its saucer, she's through the door and saying "Thanks, postie," to the postman and back again, sipping from her fine china cup and a pile of mail sitting on the table between us.

And there's a large yellow envelope on top. *Morgana Malone, La Petite Fleurette Select Patisserie and Gifterie*, it says, in Seth's medical student scrawl.

Mum opens a drawer under the table and pulls out a letter opener, handing it to me. I slice the envelope open across one end and pull out a parchment.

Morgana Malone is written across the top.

And underneath that, *to be used for 12 Singing Lessons.*

Then *Marco Garibaldi School of Singing*, under that.

I shake my head. I don't know why –

"Maybe it's a present," Mum says, looking at me over the rim of her tea cup.

I stretch under the table for my handbag and dragging it out, reach in and pull out my mobile. And there on the screen, as I breathe in the smell of wheat flour and Demerara sugar and royal icing and wine-soaked sultanas and mock cream, is the tell-tale symbol of an unopened envelope.

It's from Seth.

I click the message open.

Can we meet tonight? We need to talk.

Morgana Malone and the Riddle of the Wrong Rug

Saturday, 25th October 2014

An elastic band around his head holds an oxygen tube under Mr Rubinstein's nose. Sunk against the hospital pillows, he spreads his skinny arms out like he's welcoming the world, and beams.

"As always, I am much better for seeink your be-yooo-tiful face," he says. "Now can you brink me my liddle cap over there?" He points a shaky finger at his toupée resting on the tray table poised over the bed. "I am just a liddle bit not so naked with it on my head."

I swipe it off the tray table and hand it to him. And it's then I realise, as I feel the cloth on my fingers as he takes it from my hand, that it's cloth, it's not hairy at all.

His toupée is *cloth*. All cloth. 100%.

How did I not know that?

He plonks it on his bony head, breath rattling in his chest. "Rabbi Gutnick is comink today, so I try to look my best."

Maybe I need glasses. Because, standing here at the end of the bed, it looks very much like a toupée perched on his head. But it can't be.

"You don't want your eye patch?" I ask, though I can't see it on the tray table or on the bedside cabinet. Is the eye patch real too?

"The yarmulke is enough for Rabbi Gutnick," he says. "I don't want him to be impressed too much." And then he chuckles and his good eye twinkles. The other eye, or the darkened skin sewn over the hole where his eye once was, looks like it might be twinkling too. But what do I know, I don't know how far I can trust my eyesight.

"Is there anything I can get you?" I ask. Just what he might want, I don't know, but I'm being polite.

"You should be makink my grandson like hay until the sun shines," he says. "But instead, you come here to the hospital to visit me."

"Seth and I just weren't meant to be, Mr Rubinstein," I say. I look down at the tight hospital corners and pat the rail at the end of the bed and stretch my mouth into a smile. But no teeth though, because that would break the airtight seal and my eyelids are creating land speed records batting back the tears now.

(It's been four weeks – or four weeks and two days to be exact – since Seth's "Look, you want to get married (*but no, I don't and I've never said that*) and have children (*but when did I say that?*) and just where do you see us going? You're a sexy mama (*and you make me feel sexy, too, but not right at this very moment*) but dang! there's a lot of differences between us and hey! you're old enough to be my mother (*um, didn't I tell you that when we met?*)."

I looked at his high cheekbones on a thin face and short dark hair atop deep brown eyes and thought, *yeah, and I feel like there's an ocean of differences between us now*.)

"Ah, you will find someone else," Mr Rubinstein says, "In my heart I know this." And he taps his chest with a pale fist. "My grandson will be a *brilliant* doctor but he is also an idiot. Who could resist such *be-yooo-tiful* hair!"

I'm leaving now so there's no possibility of bumping into Seth. I fall in beside a nurse I've come to know well, our shoes squeaking on the lino as we walk down the corridor. We have something in common, though we've never spoken about it. She's growing her dye-job out too, her hair, like mine, a high-tide mark against the top of her ears.

"He's looking better without so many tubes sticking into him," I say to the nurse.

"Yes, but for how long?" she says, her squeaks peeling off into another room.

I walk to the lifts, noisy soles my only company. Pressing the DOWN button, I step back to wait for the tinny ding and the doors to open and the rest of my single life to recommence. Wiggling my toes and looking down at the floor, I wonder how many visits to Mr Rubinstein I'll make before I don't need to come here any more.

"It's not usual but it's not *unheard* of," he says. He smiles, sitting at his piano, fingers resting on the keyboard.

The studio wall behind him is filled with certificates and photos. Marco Garibaldi can sing, the certificates tell me. Marco Garibaldi can sing on a stage. Marco Garibaldi can stand with a group of people in costumes and look like a serious singer.

I *think* that's what they tell me. Because I'm not trusting my eyesight so much now after the toupée-that's-really-a-yarmulke incident this morning.

"It's not everyone whose boyfriend gives them singing lessons," Marco adds.

"*Ex*-boyfriend," I say, nodding at his deep brown eyes and curly hair and stubbly dimple in his chin. "As a breaking-up gift."

Marco smiles and nods his head. "It's a bit hard to know what to say next after you hear that."

"You could say, at least he didn't send you the bill for the lessons," I add, "because I've been asked to pay for stupider things." I'm tempted to tell him about Grigor sending me the bill for his wedding, but how silly would that make me look, still being associated with an ex who ... yeah, silly.

"Perhaps there's a song about revenge you might want to learn." Marco stands up, rifling through the sheet music piled on top of the piano.

I watch the pert curves of his bum under his shorts as he shuffles the papers about, and shake my head. "No, I don't do revenge."

The voice coming out of my mouth is scratchy and tiny and wants to run away. ("You have a wonderful voice," Seth used to say to me when, hot and wet and relaxing into the mattress after sex, I'd be singing and he'd circle my right nipple with his fingertip. "You should be a singer.")

Marco plunks away on the piano and the sounds I repeat are unrecognisable, globs and wails and whistles ending in a shriek and a gasp for salvation.

Marco's fingers stop in mid-air. "Maybe if you close your eyes," he says, dropping his hands into his lap. "Imagine yourself on a stage where the audience is smiling and appreciating the beauty of your voice as it fills the auditorium and each new note is more crystal-clear than the last."

"Or imagine I'm in a dark room where no one can see me." And then I say, noting the glassy look in his eyes, "You probably get that response all the time."

He smiles again. So much smiling and so much dimpling of that stubbly chin. "And you won't be the last."

I close my eyes and picture myself in the dark, singing. I open my mouth again and keep my eyes shut tight as Marco plunks away at the keyboard and more strangled noises slide past my tonsils and over my teeth and peter out on the floor.

And I wonder, yet again, what's on the other side of the darkness.

Morgana Malone and the Sign of the Boisterous Horse

Tuesday, 25th November 2014

"I feel as though I should read it, everybody's talking about it," her voice trills above the hushed crowd. She smiles and the brim of her black straw hat dips over one eye. She must have practiced the move hundreds of times in front of the mirror, it's so perfect, her blonde blunt-cut falling across one side of her face, and draping down across her shoulder on the other, just as her eyes look up. She laughs. Well, neighs almost, shaking her nose and mouth and whinnying. Then she points her toe and hoofs at the carpet.

Perhaps she isn't hoofing at the carpet but her hair is what I *thought* I was getting way back in January when I had mine dyed orange and bobbed. (Which is still half-grown out.) Under her straw hat her mane is sleek and lustrous.

I don't know who she is but then, I don't really know who any of these people milling and chatting and smiling and reminiscing are either.

Turning my gaze to the framed photo of Mr Rubinstein resting on the table beside the condolence book, I raise the teacup to my lips and shift my weight from my left foot to my right, with what I think is a faraway look in my eye.

Like I do this every day, this weight-shifting, faraway-looking, standing-beside-the-piano-all-on-my-very-own-looking-slightly-uncomfortable in a room with 200 other people sort of thing.

I drain the cup and place it on the saucer on the polished, upright piano, which unlike the piano Marco Garibaldi uses when he struggles to teach me singing every Saturday afternoon, is completely free of stacks of sheet music.

I can't imagine why anyone would want tinkling piano music playing as the mourners offer their condolences to the family, but then I've never been to a Jewish funeral service before so everything is novel.

"Whoa, sexy glasses," Seth says over my shoulder.

(Actually, everything is novel because with my new glasses, I'm seeing *everything* for the first time in I don't know how long.)

Seth steps around me and I breathe in his treacly cologne as his arms envelop me in a hug. It's nice to know he thinks he can still do this, eight weeks and five days after we broke up. Although "broke up" implies something that, I don't know, maybe it wasn't.

Seth looks at the grey and brown regrowth spreading across my head and says, "You are one seriously foxy woman, Morgana." And now he looks in my eyes. "And your glasses are so (and here he stops as he considers his words) ... *becoming*."

If I didn't know better I'd think he was joking, but I do know better, and a smile creeps across my face.

"Opi would be very happy you're here," he adds, with just the vaguest, slightest, tugging catch at the end. His eyes are ringed red and the tip of his nose is pink and I look at the high cheekbones on his thin face and short dark hair atop deep brown eyes and I am struck again by how much he looks like Grigor. Even Grigor after his plastic surgery.

And I can't help it, it just flies out of my mouth. "Mr Rubinstein was a wonderful man and he adored you."

Seth smiles, that 1000-watt grin he flashes the moment he first wakes up. "Yeah, well, he was *Opi* and he was special."

"He was, he always made visiting him in hospital fun."

We both nod, hands clasped in front of us, like some sort of mirror-action game.

"Are you seeing anyone?" he asks.

I want to say, *And your grandfather loved how polite you always are asking after people* but instead I lie. "Yes, no, well ... you know, sort of, it's ... (and here I shrug) ... early days."

"Yeah, me too."

I don't really want to hear that so I listen for any other sound floating around the room, which happens to be the horse-woman saying, "I'm only becoming a doctor so it will make me a better mother." Followed by a trilling bray.

Seth says something else to me – something like well, it's great to see you or have a nice life or please sign the guestbook or I hope you're enjoying the singing lessons I gave you as a breaking-up gift (or maybe he says goodbye gift) – and I nod (again) and he walks through the crowd which shows no sign of leaving, to the other side of the room and sidles up beside horse-woman and slips his arm around her waist.

Hmm, so there's a downside to being able to see better.

"If I don't have a baby soon I think my ovaries are going to burst," horse-woman says to a man in a yarmulke.

A dark suit steps into my line of vision so I bend at the waist and through the crowd, watch horse-woman slip her arm around Seth. He nuzzles his chin into her shoulder and I wish I could dislike her but ... they look quite good together. He's a little shorter than her and she's older than him – maybe thirty, maybe she was a nurse before she started studying medicine, or a hair / hat model in a previous life, or a jockey before she grew too tall – but physically they look in proportion.

Still, I wonder what Seth sees in her. And even more so, listening to her conversation and watching her cock her head and drape her sleek and lustrous mane, and pose.

And I wonder what he ever saw in me. Just an older woman pity fu –

"How are you, Susan?"

I turn to see Barry, Grigor's brother, just as he takes a blini from a tray offered by a waitress wearing crisp black and a crisper smile.

"*Morgana*, I mean Morgana," Barry adds, as the waitress disappears with her tray into the crowd.

Barry, whose high cheekbones on a thin face and short dark hair atop deep brown eyes also remind me of Grigor. Grigor before his plastic surgery. Grigor before he had his nose chiselled and his wrinkles blasted away.

Barry, who I worked for a few months back, in the therapy practice he shares with Grigor and who had appointments with Mr Rubinstein almost every day, which is how I came to know Mr Rubinstein in the first place and how I came to be here at Mr Rubinstein's funeral.

"*Susan* is okay," I say. "It's my real name."

Barry – his mouth full of blini (the half uneaten portion he clasps in his fingers as he waves his hand in the air) – looks at me, eyes shining with new interest. And swallows.

"You're just not a Morgana to me, you're always a Susan. I never worked out why you changed it."

Oh, it was another life ago ...

"How's Grigor?" I ask. (God, I can't help myself, I don't *care* how Grigor is yet I still do the polite thing and ask about him.)

"Fuck him, fuck whatever his name is even if he is my twin brother," Barry says. "Fuck him if he's just got out of prison. How are *you*? *Really*, I mean. I want to know: how are you *really*?"

And now the blini and napkin are on the piano beside my empty teacup and he's flinging his hands in the air.

"I mean, I'm a little late for the wedding rehearsal and suddenly I'm not best man any longer and you're not matron of honour and the wedding is off and I'm told you've resigned your admin job at the practice and I have no idea what's happened and I really enjoyed having you in the office ..."

I smile. His intense unblinking gaze might put some people off but I've always liked that about him, even when he was my brother-in-law, even when Grigor was still called Greg. And Barry's enthusiastic hand-waving is infectious, another mirror-game. I'm stirring the air too and I don't know why.

"... and now here you are," he adds, with a sigh and a smile, "ready to tell me."

I don't know what to tell him.

"But it's old news, isn't it?" Barry says. "*Old* news." He picks up what's left of the blini and the napkin from the piano and looks around the room. Perhaps Jewish funerals are popular, because the room is still full, and shows no signs of emptying soon. Even with heartbreak, I think, something can be learned.

"I guess Mr Rubinstein must have been one of your favourite patients," I say.

"Favourite patient?" Barry says. "God no, he was my favourite *bookie*." He laughs, like he's been caught with his hand in the biscuit jar and is trying to charm his way out with disarming honesty. "And not a great bookie either but he was a nice man and nice men his age and with his life experience are few and far between."

I nod. And Barry waves his hands in the air a little more.

"But he was never my patient, he was too switched-on for psychotherapy."

I nod again, just as I see the horse-woman pass behind Barry, swiping the straw hat from her head as she smiles. And there I see it, in broad daylight, or as broad as daylight gets inside well-attended funeral refreshments at a well-appointed funeral home: her very own racing stripe, dark brown regrowth through the blonde mane.

A smile spreads across my face. Somehow that regrowth makes me feel better.

Morgana Malone and the Promise of 1000 Tomorrows

Thursday, 25th December 2014

"One big fantastic time we be having," Ludmilla says. Greasy grey-brown hair sticking out from under her bearskin hat, she sucks on her Christmas cigar. Clouds of eau de old-shoes-left-for-too-long-in-a-mouldy-wardrobe puff past my face.

"Christmas in July in June? No!" Now Ludmilla stomps her feet on the grey paving then throws her arms out like she's about to break into a show tune. "No no no! Christmas in December in Paris!"

Who would have thought?

Paris!

with Ludmilla!!

on Christmas Day!!!

Through my glasses, the high, wide entryway on the opposite side of the Louvre courtyard grows closer and closer with each stride.

I am not interested in why my former housemate and fortune teller is trying to be amusing. Nor am I interested in her wheezing or why she smokes celebratory cigars on Christmas Day. All I want to do is fasten the padlock on the famous Pont des Arts, then throw the key in the Seine. A photo of the padlock on the mesh railing glistening in the winter sun would be a bonus, but my camera is nestled in my suitcase back in our twin share at the Hotel d'Arabesque so I'm not counting on anything. It's just bridge, lock, throw. Anything else is a miracle.

I pick up speed, heels scuffing on the grey stones louder and louder and faster and faster.

The padlock weighs down the pocket of my puffy beige coat, banging a rhythm against my leg. And my fingertips are pink through fingerless gloves as I stride through the covered entryway, beneath hundreds of years of history (not that I'm interested in any of them), and step outside the Louvre. Ahead, I can see the famous pedestrian bridge and only metres away, catch a glimpse of the river.

"Wait!" Ludmilla calls out behind me. "Why you hurry? Bridge is falling down?"

I resist the urge to hurl a crack over my shoulder about this being Paris, not London, but western European bridge jokes are probably beyond her.

She's still yabbering on. "Stop! Why you be the bitch who stole Christmas?!"

God? fate? traffic? is with me as looking straight ahead I step off the kerb, no glance left or right, and onto the zebra crossing. My hair is short now, the leftover orange bob gone, chopped out, replaced with a brown and grey-streaked au naturel pixie cut, an early Christmas gift / holiday surprise / life-is-really-good celebration I gave myself two days ago. The puffy collar is warm against my neck as I hunker inside the coat.

And I'm charging, heels echoing on the black and white stripes and Ludmilla, who has kept me company ever since we left Adelaide at 10.35 last night, flying Emirates to Bahrain and then to Charles de Gaulle Airport, her gasps and wheezes and coughs grow fainter with each stride.

("No wondering no sheikhs are coming here," Ludmilla said as she sat beside me on the Emirates flight. "You looking like Lebanese butcher." Then I shuddered as her hand ran up the back of my hair. "Your head is full of pricks.")

Bridge. Lock. Throw.

I will have a bruise on my thigh from the padlock bashing against it – the padlock's large and gold, though not gold just golden, maybe brass, maybe just wrapped in gold foil, I don't know but it *looks* gold and it has our names engraved on it.

Perhaps if I keep walking I can make London by sundown, or sundown tomorrow given it's winter and it gets dark by 5:00pm according to the internet.

Maybe I can escape Ludmilla.

Last night, I caught a cab to Adelaide Airport. *Meet me inside the international departure lounge,* Barry's text had said.

My armpits were sticky with the summer heat as I walked through the echoey terminal. And a grin spread across my face as all other travellers' noise faded away and I saw Barry standing outside the Customs check-in, in profile, high cheekbones on a thin face and short dark hair atop deep brown eyes.

But then he turned and it wasn't Barry, it was Grigor. His twin. Cheeks smoother than Barry's, nose finer than Barry's, forehead blander than Barry's ... and he smiled when he saw me.

"Morgana," Grigor said, "it's good you could make it."

(What else was I going to do? On our two-week anniversary Barry bent down on one knee and said, deep brown eyes looking straight into mine, "Susan, you can sing carols at Christmas dinner for my homeless mates at the Whitmore Square Shelter, and I'll organise a screen for you to stand behind so you won't see their faces watching you while you sing" – which was tempting – "or we can fly to Paris on Christmas Eve and have croissants by the Seine on Christmas Day. You choose.")

"Where's Barry?" I asked. I would have fluffed my new hair except it's so short there isn't much to fluff and my hands were full holding my new puffy coat (bought just for Paris) and my carry-on luggage heavy with the three layers of winter clothes I'd packed to change into on the plane.

"In hospital," Grigor said, his deep brown eyes looking straight into mine. "Having a bit of a Christmas episode."

And then I saw Ludmilla standing behind Grigor, just as Grigor took my hand in his. Which was awkward as it was my left hand, half-buried under the puffy coat.

"Barry's fear of flying and of being trapped in confined spaces for a long time have taken their usual toll and he's having a rest on the psych ward," Grigor said. "It's a Christmas tradition. Although his fear of tinsel is new."

121

The puffy coat slid off my arm. "Barry flies to Paris every Christmas?" I looked down at the coat, pooled at my feet.

Grigor nodded. "He attempts to, yes. Barry's trip to Paris is a work in progress."

My hand slipped out of Grigor's clasp, just as Ludmilla peeked over his shoulder. "Barry ask me to Paris to go for him," she said.

"But I was with Barry this morning. We picked up my new passport together."

Grigor patted my hand. "Barry knows how to manage his illness. He knew weeks ago this would happen. And you can't fault his psychotherapy training, he recognises the signs."

"Barry give this for you," Ludmilla added, and handed me the padlock and key. The padlock was engraved with *Barry and Susan 25.12.14*, inside a heart. "He say, Tell Susan, Go! So I think you be this Susan."

I bent down to pick up the puffy coat. As I grabbed it, I saw a shiny new red and yellow overnight bag on the floor beside Ludmilla's feet. I stood up. "So this was all planned?"

"Go," Grigor said. "Don't even question it Morgana, just go." And then he added, "What other plans do you have for Christmas anyway?"

I did not expect to share my first visit to the most romantic city on Earth with Ludmilla. But maybe, while we were having our Christmas croissants by the Seine, I thought, I could give her the slip. Maybe push her in the river.

I opened my carry-on bag, took out my boarding pass and passport, and snapped it shut. I stepped around Ludmilla.

"I noticed your hair is no longer the colour of my favourite vegetable," Grigor said behind me.

I shuffled into the queue for Customs.

"It looks very attractive," Grigor said, "and not that masculine when you become used it."

Smiling at the woman in blue, I handed her my passport and boarding pass.

Thousands of padlocks glimmer in the muted sun.

Bridge. Lock. Throw.

My footsteps slow as I walk the Pont des Arts, wooden planks scuffing beneath my feet as I search the mesh railings for a spot for the padlock. The padlock in my coat pocket, banging against my leg and creating a bruise. The padlock Barry gave to Ludmilla, because he fears flying and cramped spaces and Christmas tinsel – haven't seen any tinsel in Paris so far, though I've really been too angry to look – to make the trip he'd planned for us both.

Bridge. Lock. Throw.

I thrust my hand inside the coat pocket. The padlock, key inside it, is cold against my fingertips. My eyes dart around the bridge, around the other pedestrians, searching searching searching the railings for a spot.

Bridge, lock, throw.

I spot a spot big enough to manoeuvre the lock into. Stepping up to the rail, I look over my shoulder towards the Louvre. Ludmilla, breasts bobbing, is heaving towards me.

This was supposed to be my moment with Barry.

bridge-lock-throw

And I don't want to share any more of this moment with Ludmilla.

bridgelockthrow

I'm standing on the bridge.

Bridge.

I pull the padlock out of my pocket, gold key still wedged inside it.

Lock.

The padlock is open so I snap it shut. I pull out the key. I see *Barry and Susan 25.12.14*, surrounded by the engraved heart.

Throw.

I swing my arm back and throw the padlock over the rail.

Throw.

I throw the padlock off the bridge.

Throw.

I throw the padlock off the bridge and into the river.

Throw.

I don't even hear the faintest plop as the padlock hits the water.

I look down. The key glimmers in my hand.

My head snaps back towards the Louvre. Ludmilla has stopped walking. Her mouth is open. Perhaps she is dribbling, or perhaps it is too cold to dribble. Either way, she is not saying anything and she is standing stock still, fur boots nailed to the wooden planks of the Pont des Arts.

My mouth is open too. But the insides of my cheeks are dry and my tongue is cold, so I close my lips and wait, arms by my sides. I think I might be pouting.

Burrowing into the neck of my coat again, I pull my bottom lip over my top lip and breathe out, my mouth a funnel, fogging up my glasses.

I can't see through the fog.

VOLUMES

These stories were all written for print anthologies *Pure Slush* published in 2011, 2012 and 2013.

Pure Slush anthologies always have a theme, usually referenced in the title of the complete book. So, *Espresso* is from *slut*; *I'd go with the shotgun* is from *Notausgang: emergency exit*; *One More Chance* is from *obit.*; *A Little Squirming* is from *Catherine refracted*; and *Caplitalist Bastard* is from *barcode*.

Key Meeting and *Lamington Drive* are both from *gorge*, a novel in stories all set on the one day in a Maine restaurant.

Espresso

Other seated customers fade into the background. And I watch his face as, with each breath, the crucifix rises and falls on my pecs.

He looks up and I catch his gaze.

I smile, steal a glance towards the kitchen – morning radio playing, cook and kitchenhand in their blur of work – then press the button, rinse the coffee filter under the jet of hot water, and watch the steam rise.

"How much is it?" he asks.

"Three eighty," I say.

He follows the twinkling gold prickling against my chest stubble.

I glance past him and note a newly vacant table. "Stacy," I say, nodding at the table.

Stacy – nineteen, set chin and damp armpits – rushes over to clear it.

I flick fresh coffee into the filter, stamp it as its aroma, strong and potent and dark, hits my nostrils, then lock the filter in place on the espresso machine.

He smiles, I assume at my wrist control.

Placing a cup on the metal tray, pausing before I press the button to let the boiling water filter through, I look up again into his swarthy face.

"Has it started to rain?" I ask. "I finish in half an hour. I want to go for a run."

A quick turn of the head off to the kitchen again then I press the button, whirring the machine into action.

He looks at me with deep brown eyes and what must be the longest eyelashes I have seen all day – and I've been looking.

"On and off," he says. He closes his mouth – sandy-pink lips, even teeth, strong jawline – then opens it again and adds the clincher: "Intermittently."

So he's not a street sweeper and if he is, he's probably studying at night so he can go to university. Looking at his crisp white t-shirt (I can't see much beyond his moulded chest and flat stomach without craning over the counter), he's probably off to the gym after this too.

Stacy rushes behind me, lean arms laden with cups and plates, and starts talking in the kitchen.

I press the button again and the machine stops. Opening the fridge under the counter, I take out the plastic bottle of milk, pour some into a stainless steel jug, replace the bottle, close the door and thrust the jug under the steamer wand, the steamer's tip resting just below the milk's lip.

"So, that was a cappuccino for you and a ... ?"

He rests his hands on the counter top and I see the fine hair on his ringless fingers. "Just the cappuccino, thanks."

He turns to check his nearby seat, bag slung over a chair, and newspaper and keys laying on the table.

As I rotate the metal jug around the wand, whirling the milk into froth and bubble, I press my hips against the counter top and feel my cock growing inside my jeans. And pull away, hoping he can – despite the angle of the counter and the machine and the café rush – see the maturing bulge.

I breathe in – almost a gasp, loud enough for him to hear – and the crucifix rises and falls again. Flicking the machine off, I withdraw the milk from the wand and sneak another glance towards the kitchen.

More noise and mixing and chopping.

The front door opens and a young mother wheels a baby in a pusher into the café.

Placing the cup on the counter top, I spiral the milk over the shot of coffee. Metal scrapes against metal as I scoop the last froth from the jug and spoon it over the cup.

I grab the shaker of chocolate.

An eye on movement in the kitchen – are they swinging along to the radio? – I pull a small stencil, round and metal, out of my pocket, and hover it over the froth. Shaking the chocolate in quick movements above it, breathing in his cologne as he leans forward to watch my handiwork, the ten digits of my mobile number magically appear in brown.

I push the stencil into my back pocket and feel my fingers through the fabric.

The cup now on the saucer, I push it towards him, slowly looking from my mobile number, under my eyebrows, and up.

He looks, matching mine.

Breathing in, my chest puffs out and I turn to the young mother. She looks tired and smells of baby. "What would you like?"

He slides the cappuccino off the counter and takes it to his table.

"A skinny capp and an apple juice, please."

I busy myself wiping down the espresso machine, the counter top, the fridge door, killing time as I listen, cloth damp in my hand.

Stacy rushes behind me carrying two bowls of soup, perspiration beading on her forehead.

The young mother bends down to her baby in the pusher. "I'm just getting you some apple juice," she says. "The man is just getting it for you."

I look over at him. His t-shirt sculpts across his shoulders and over his biceps and my cock stirs again. He turns in the chair and I see an erect nipple in profile. My focus dims and I see him fucking me against a tree, my running shorts around my ankles, my arms rubbing against rough bark as I bend forward, hugging the trunk as he fingers open my hole and pounds me with his hard, thick veiny cock.

I watch as he reaches into his pocket.

The baby cries.

"We don't have straight apple juice," I say to the young mother. I turn around and look into the drinks fridge. "But we have apple and guava and apple and passionfruit."

She wrinkles her face. "Do you have apple and peach?"

"No," I say, peering further through the glass doors. "But we do have peach and apple."

She screws up her nose again. "What's the difference?"

"Less apple and more peach," I guess.

My hip pocket vibrates.

I look through the window and see Stacy at the tables outside, writing orders on her pad.

"Bruno!" I call into the kitchen.

Bruno looks up from his place at the bench. Already he is wiping his hands on his apron.

"I'll go," says my wife, working beside him.

Bruno settles back to chopping mushrooms as my wife, untying the strings, tosses her apron on a stool and walks up to the counter.

I duck into the storeroom, pull my mobile from my hip pocket, flick it open.

U still going 4 that run?

Stacy rushes back into the kitchen. And I look through the doorway, past my wife serving at the counter, over the espresso machine. And into his eyes as he stands up.

I nod.

I'd go with the shotgun

"I'd go with the shotgun," she says. "It's not as neat but it gets the job done quicker."

I adore Vi. My favourite ex-aunt, she dyes her hair Mortician's Siren (so the packet says) and we meet up once in a full moon, when her sideshow and my job – touring drag show or touring magic show or dead body in a police re-enactment for country TV – find us in the same town.

She sells tickets to three different rides and as she says, "They're as cheap as shit but even I look good at night when the light's behind me."

Her boss quivers on the floor of the ticketing booth, hands tied behind his back with my pink-and-purple keep fit skipping rope. I point a liquorice gun at his shivering forehead. Sweat drips from under his bri-nylon toupée and courses across his cheeks. I'm surprised the gun hasn't melted down his nose.

"You'd better hand over all the money you owe her," I say, gravel-voiced, my dead body make-up from that day's re-enactment cracking in the moonlight streaming through the window. I wave the gun at him, hoping the smell of fear masks the smell of liquorice.

I kick his leg, forgetting I'm also half-dressed for my drag act – they only wanted a medium shot so to save time I'm full glamour from the waist down – and stub my big toe through my open stiletto.

"This isn't going very well," Vi says, and she pulls me across, just a mincing step really, to the other side of the booth. "We should've done this last night when he had the weekend's takings. Monday's our slowest day."

I look through the window. In the distance, I can see the last stragglers stumbling through the Winifred Maude Chambers Memorial Gate, letters stencilled backwards against the night. I sigh. Country fairs and faded sideshows and drunks staggering in the moonlight: you can taste the old-fashioned romance.

I sniff.

"We better finish him off soon," Vi adds. "His wife's probably expecting him home for tea."

There's a clatter as the old man, knee bent near his chest, kicks his false teeth across the floor. (They fell out when I pushed him into the booth.) "You're a fuckin' fweakthow!" he yells. "You'll never get away with thith!"

I snap his jaw down, click my tongue like I'm cocking the gun and shove the liquorice deep into his open mouth. His eyes bog with fear and he gurgles and chokes.

I grab the cloth bag I think has the money inside it, and kick his shin again. Then I snatch my vinylette hold-all from the counter, sling it over my shoulder as I throw open the door and I'm outside, stilettoes thundering on the dirt.

Vi wheezes behind me.

"When's the next bus?" I call out to her. "They'll never look for us there."

"Jeez, I don't feel so good," Vi says, gulping big breaths behind me. "I think I need a bit of a lie down ..."

I listen to catch the rest but she falls smack against a car and her voice disappears as the car alarm, loud and foggy, blasts the night air.

But my head is light and my heart is pumping and pulling my Farrah wig from my vinylette hold-all and cramming it on my head, I run past the THIS WAY OUT sign and through the Winifred Maude Chambers Memorial Gate. I'm like Butch Cassidy and the Smoky Bandit, high heels clacking on the lumpy asphalt.

Life is bumpy at the best of times, but as I round the Victoria Hotel and charge up Murray Street, the night air streaming through my Farrah wig, I stuff the cloth bag into my hold-all and laugh: sometimes you just have to take what God gives you.

Key Meeting

"Did you swallow?"

Mya turns to look through the patio windows into the main room of the restaurant, then tilts her head back and blows cigarette smoke through her nostrils. "Of course I did." She looks at me, caressing the skin on her neck and above her breasts in that constant way she does, and plays with her ugly necklace with that tennis ball on the end. "We were in the parking lot."

"I've seen him around town," I say. "He looks like a real gusher." I spoon Key Lime pie – tart and sweet and creamy and tangy – into my mouth, and chew, savouring the taste across my tongue. I would gargle it if I could, but the moment isn't mine.

Elbow resting on the tablecloth, Mya cups her chin in her hand, squashing her jowls over her thumb and index finger and sending the wrinkles around her eyes into orbit. "I didn't want anyone to see me," she says. Smoke curls around her hair from the stub wedged between her fingers. "I don't want to get a reputation."

"No," I say. My grey bob brushes my cheeks as I lick the back of the spoon. "Not after all this time."

Mya tosses her cigarette on the patio and grinds it out with her heel. "Isn't that why I pay you?" she says. "To protect me from my own spin?"

I can feel her hot ashy breath on my face as I pick up a glass of water, ice cubes clinking as I hold it to my mouth. The spoon hangs in mid-air in my other hand. "I'm not just your therapist, Mya. I need to see other patients to make money."

I sip the water, put the glass down, place the spoon on the plate with a clink, and wipe my mouth with the crisp edge of the table napkin.

"That was delicious."

And napkin to mouth, swallow a tiny, tangy burp.

"Can I have some more?"

"Yes, Aileen," Mya says, voice trailing off with the afternoon breeze. "If we have any more left, you may."

My eyes, dark and hooded and shrouded in aloof professionalism, burn as I watch her profile, now surveying the calm waters of Libby Cove. My hand itches to reach over and slap her across the face. How many times does the bitch have to be told? We don't say *may I* when requesting something in Australia, we say *can I* or *could I. Fuck you, cum-gobbling whore!* I want to say. Just think yourself lucky you don't have to establish a new therapy practice every time your husband lands a new job in a strange place. In a strange country. In a strange time zone. Studying diseased fucking fish, of all things. When there's nothing else to do and besides, you're not trained for anything but listening to ugly women whine about their sad, pathetic, provisional lives.

But I sit instead, saying nothing, waiting for the pie to arrive – placed in front of me at an incredibly slow pace by the lazy cow with the frozen face – then gaze at it, as I'm sure it's half the size of the previous piece.

"May I have a new spoon, please?" I say. And smile up at Kimberley's blank bovine expression. Kimberley smiles – well, she would smile, if she could manage it – and walks back inside.

"So what did it taste like?" I ask Mya. "Italian cum usually tastes like bad mozzarella."

Mya looks away, like she wants to be anywhere – anywhere! – but here having to contend with unmotivated staff. Luckily, she maintains her cool and resists the temptation for flight. I've been telling her to let bygones be bygones and fire Kimberley for weeks.

The girl returns with a new spoon, albeit a smudged one – my face is a dirty blur in the reflection – and as she takes the first plate and spoon away, I dig into the fresh piece. "Yu shdn bsozntdzbuoonnz," I say.

"Don't talk with your mouth full, Aileen."

I swallow and put the spoon down, refusing to let her foul mood change mine. "You know what would be good? A glass of New Zealand sauvignon blanc to wash it down, preferably from the Marlborough region."

Palms down on the table, Mya stands up, steps around the next table, and shielding her eyes from the soft afternoon sun with her hands, looks out across the water. I can't be bothered with this silly performance, and turn to look through the windows into the restaurant. Inside her brother darts between tables, trying to look busy.

But I see her reflected in the window and can't resist. "Penny for your thoughts."

I watch Mya put a hand – again – on her enormous cleavage and breathe out. I have seen her do this so many times I have it timed to the millisecond. "I think our time together is coming to an end," she says.

I stop, mouth stuffed with Key Lime filling and crumbling crust. I swallow, put my spoon down again, cough to clear my throat, and turn. Mya still has her back to me.

"You came to me two years ago crying for help," I say. "After Alex left you for that Bulgarian whore, you were so afraid of real intimacy you couldn't go near a cock. And now you're swallowing, even if it is for the *wrong* reason." I pick up my spoon again. "Excuse me for pushing you back on your back with your legs spread."

Mya spins around so fast her jowls wobble and threaten to splat on the patio.

"You didn't swallow his load because you wanted the feeling," I jump in, waving the spoon at her. "You did it because you wanted it *finished!*"

I thrust the spoon under what's left of the pie.

"You probably stroked his chin and made cooing noises and desperate double entendres and clicking sounds with your clitoris," I add, lifting the last of the pie to my mouth. "But really, your mind was a thousand miles away, and you were just using him to shore up your sorry need for affirmation."

Mya winces in the light. Is she focussing on someone inside the restaurant – her silly brother Robert or kiss-of-death Kimberley – or just avoiding eye contact? But I refuse to let her get away with this behaviour.

I swallow the last delicious morsel, and the chair scrapes on the slate as I stand up, smoothing my white blouse over my white skirt with my free hand.

"And you know the only person in this entire frigid state who can bother being honest with you is me, Mya.

You get a two-for-one deal with me: therapist *and* friend. And you say our time is coming to an end," I mimic, mouth pursed and head bobbing.

I throw the spoon down, sit back in the chair and grab the glass, ice clinking.

"Still, swallowing *is* progress, I'll give you that."

Mya blinks.

"I hope you enjoyed the taste."

I look out across the water and sniff the breeze. It smells of salt and seaweed and far away dreams.

"What a lovely day," I say, and pressing my lips together, I hum.

Mya sits down at the other table and crosses her knees. A pinched look about her cheeks, I can't tell if she's crying or hungry.

"It was never my idea to see you," she says, head hanging, voice soft. "Alex said if I got help he'd think about coming back."

I bend down in the chair, looking up at her face as she concentrates on her shoes. I grab the spoon again and jab the air. "Alex only ever did two good things for you: left you with this restaurant and introduced you to me. And we still don't know if you can make this place turn a profit."

With a stab to the heart, I know I've got her. Mya doesn't have a head for business, despite her talk of managing art galleries and promotional outcomes and expanding commercial opportunities. Too many people are getting fat on her bottom line.

For the first time since our session started Mya looks me in the eye. "Robert says we should expand but I wake up every morning wanting to throw all my Jimmy Choos in a suitcase and head back to New York."

I want to reach out, crush her head to my bosom and coo that everything will be okay. But I know my professional boundaries.

"Hey," I say, looking through the windows into the restaurant and seeing a figure perch on a stool at the bar. "Maybe you can get some guy to cream your cleavage this time. Looks like Happy Hour's about to start."

Lamington Drive

If you could look inside the staff restroom window at Café Gano now, what would you see? A therapist in her late 40's (if she's having a good day), sitting on the tiled floor, legs splayed, white skirt hitched up around her waist, pink high-heeled sandals on her feet, handbag open on the floor, white blouse with half the buttons undone.

"Mya!" she's probably calling out. "My-yaaa!" Well, in her head she's calling out. But since Mya slipped her that Roofie and then locked the restroom door behind her, Aileen's brain and mouth are not in sync and yes, the therapist on the floor is dribbling down her chin.

And what's running through her head? As her mind spins and her mouth gurgles and her eyes focus in and out on the locked door, she's back in Australia, back in her grandmother's kitchen in Kingston Park making lamingtons for the church lamington drive.

Lamingtons?

You will need:

- some vanilla sponge cake
- powdered cocoa, icing sugar and water, for

the chocolate icing

• desiccated coconut.

Grandma's kitchen faces west, looking across the Gulf St Vincent, over the cliff and down onto the Kingston Park Caravan Park and the sandy beach. It's Australia, where all the beaches are sand – and *only* sand. The idea of a beach without sand is, well ... foreign! And it's her childhood Aileen's remembering so of course the sun is shining and the sky is blue and there are no clouds, none at all (not like Maine) and everything is bright and clear and warm and open.

Aileen, with sleep-tousled hair and her white summer nightie caught in the waistband of her pants – Aileen has learned to call them *panties* when she goes underwear shopping in the States – yawns as she walks into the kitchen. She's eight or ten but in her forties too, as you are in hallucinations, and she sidles up to Grandma who, holding a large metal bowl, stops her stirring of the chocolate mix of cocoa powder and icing sugar and water: with so many lamingtons to make, so much chocolate icing to dip the cake into, so much coconut to spread on plates for rolling the cake across, she's been up since 7:00am. Though mostly reading the newspaper and washing the dishes and sweeping the floor and eating breakfast and doing everything to avoid making lamingtons.

"Good morning, Leenie," Grandma says as she puts the bowl down, and the child / adult Aileen sinks against Grandma's side and allows Grandma to snake her arm around her and draw her close. With her noted sweet tooth, it's surprising it took her granddaughter so long to smell the sugar and get out of bed.

"Can I help you?" Aileen asks, sniffing the sweet chocolate and her grandmother's Softasilk hand creme as Grandma leans down and kisses the top of her head. So Aileen's young enough to want to do things all the time, help Grandma, please her and earn her affection, do things *with* her. Even though she's barely awake and still yawning. Even though not too many years later, she will find Grandma a little average really, just a bit plain and boring and unsophisticated.

A bit like lamingtons, now she thinks of it.

Grandma's kitchen is infused with light, much like the white-tiled staff restroom. The kitchen blind is pulled up to reveal the perfect blue-and-white day, the flounces of the white nylon café curtains framing the perfect view. Magpies caw and waves lap on the beach far below which you can just hear when you crane your head and strain your ears west.

Shifting her lamington-making utensils about, Grandma watches Aileen out of the corner of her eye. Early mornings are touch and go: Aileen's moods depend on the wind and the sun and TV programming and the colour of the bedsheets and the cool of the lino and the smell of the air. And now she's scowling.

Aileen scratches her head. Aileen scratches her tummy. Aileen puts her arms around Grandma's waist and yawns and smiles and Grandma smiles and picks up the bowl again. Aileen watches Grandma's deft wrist action, the chocolate mix whisking and scraping around the metal as she adds more cocoa and icing sugar and water then more cocoa and icing sugar and water then more again.

Some people cut the lamingtons in half and spread raspberry jam inside, sticking the two halves together before icing them, but Ida – that's Aileen's grandmother – thinks it spoils a good lamington. The church has asked Ida to make sixty – they're all pre-sold – and everyone knows that while Ida makes a good lamington, she never fills them with jam.

Lamington snobs think the absence of jam inside the lamington means it's not a proper lamington. Ida thinks the absence of jam makes for more time to spend doing almost anything else today.

But Ida is also a jam snob. She will only use homemade, and she stopped making her own jam four years ago, when Aileen was six or eight or in her early 40's.

"Can I help you, Grandma?"

"Are you sure you're awake enough?" Grandma laughs.

Leenie nods.

"You don't want breakfast first?"

Leenie shakes her head.

"Well, pull the stool up here and we can make them together." Ida smiles. She wishes she wasn't such a capable cook. Then she wouldn't be roped into making them every year by the over-officious church fundraising committee, with or without raspberry jam. Soon enough she'll learn to say *no, my relationship with God does not include lamingtons*. But that's some time away still.

Metal feet scrape on the kitchen lino as Aileen drags the stool across to the kitchen bench.

I should really get her to wash her hands Ida thinks, as Aileen sits down on the stool, vinyl oomphing. But imagining the faces of the church fundraising committee ladies Ida smiles again, watching Aileen rub sleep from her eyes, and says nothing.

Ida has already placed a large plate on the bench. Putting aside the bowl of chocolate icing again, she takes out a pair of scissors from a drawer, snips off the corner of the plastic packet laying beside the plate, and pours a mound of the desiccated coconut onto it. The sweet smells of summer and the tropics and Christmas in a warmer climate fill their nostrils.

"Is that coconut?" Aileen asks.

"Yes," Ida nods.

Ida reaches up and from on top of the fridge, takes down two cake tins. There's the release of the vacuumed whoop as she works the lid off the first, then the metal clang as she puts the lid on the bench. Lifting out a round sponge cake made yesterday (made today would be too fresh), she places it on a wooden chopping board. And with a large sharp knife, slices the cake into strips, then the strips into cubes, her other hand as light on the sponge as the sponge itself, no impression or indent or pothole left behind. The triangles at the ends will become lamingtons, yes, but for dessert tonight or afternoon tea or the cook's trade-off this morning.

Aileen watches, eyes still half-lidded, and yawns again.

Back in the staff restroom, more dribble runs down her chin.

"It's good we're doing this now," Ida says, placing a wire cake rack beside the plate of coconut. "You'll need a bath after this."

"I don't have baths now," Aileen corrects. "Only showers. I haven't had a bath in thirty years."

"A shower it is then," says Ida, who takes a cube of sponge cake and drops it in the chocolate icing. Aileen watches Ida roll the cube in the chocolate, spooning icing over the top for better coverage, then picks it up, dripping, in her fingers, and plops it on the coconut. Then she rolls the wet sponge in the coconut, spooning coconut over the top for better coverage, picks it up and shakes it over the plate, then places it with care on the wire cake rack. Already icing and coconut glob on her fingers.

"You want to do the coconut?" Grandma asks.

Aileen nods, and they start a chain, a slow procession, Grandma on the chocolate, Aileen on the coconut. It would have been much quicker if Grandma did it alone, but that's not what's happening in Aileen's head.

But outside a lawnmower starts up – this is suburbia after all – its roar cracking open the quiet morning. Aileen stands up on the stool – "What are you doing?" her grandmother asks, as Aileen's nightie is still caught in the waistband of her pants – and waves, her arm through the open window, which isn't really open as all windows have flyscreens on them, but she waves through the open window anyway.

Grandad is outside, and the sound of the throbbing lawnmower and the pounding waves on the sandy beach and the cawing magpies and the puttputt of a joy boat on Libby Cove and the screech of rubber leave boring old lamingtons for dead.

One More Chance

"This is nuts," I said.

Web looked at me with rheumy eyes and coughed, dislodging the mucous in his throat. He blinked, his voice soft and apologetic. "But I've got the bug."

I shook my head and though I try to avoid melodramatic gestures during working hours, put my head in my hands and stared at the grain on my desk. "It doesn't make any sense, Web."

"Just one more chance," he said. And maybe there was a sniff too, I can't be sure: I was looking at a knot in the formica, the swirl in the fake wood mirroring my own churning thoughts.

"I need this, Jimmy." And yes, there was a definite sniff this time. The bastard had me.

You know the drill – give me a lost cause and I'm donating my life's savings, my wife's savings and all the sperm we have hiding in the freezer for a rainy day. "Have you told Esther?"

Web smiled – what was he by then? Sixty-five? seventy? ninety even? – and I saw a brown tooth out of the corner of my eye: remember I was still officially head down, looking at the wood grainette.

"How can I send you out there with those teeth?" I said, breath hot in my palms, peering at him through embarrassed fingers. "This is the age of cosmetology. You need a Hollywood grin just to get work understudying a hat-check girl."

Web pulled his upper lip over his teeth. (My heart leaped inside my chest.) Then he added the clincher: "Do you want me to get down on my knees?" And wincing in pain, he inched towards the edge of the leatherette chair. Which was louder: the grind in the chair or the creak in his hips?

"No, I don't want you to get down on your knees," I said. I thought my heart would explode! So I stood up and flicking aside the plastic wash-and-wipe curtains, looked out the grimy window. What was out there? (Is it worth remembering?) Some well-meaning suits crossing the street nine floors down, on their way to lives and careers and whatever else it is they do – or did – with more purpose.

How far can you take being cruel to be kind?

"There's always the borscht belt," I said. "Though the belt's a bit tighter than it used to be."

Web's voice cheered in my ears like a pep squad. "The borscht belt sounds like a great place to start."

"Or the Mortgage Belt," I added. "Or the Commuter Belt. Or the fan belt." I turned and looked at this upstanding citizen and wealthy philanthropist (though who ever heard of a poor philanthropist?) who just didn't have what it took to make it in the world of comedy. But who sipped at the infectious showbiz cup like half the other half-wits in this half-whacked world.

"But I have a new act," Web offered, hands open, like Al Jolson in confession. "And I've been slaying them at the seniors' home." His eyes glazed, maybe at the memory.

My own eyes searched the ceiling. "Web, they're laughing at the same jokes every time because they can't remember them from last week." I closed my eyes and pushed my arms out, standing like a crucifix. With a vague puff I'd probably fall backwards through the window and crash onto the street below.

Web dropped into what must have been his seniors' home routine. "Why did the chicken cross the road?"

"But Web, Web, Web," I said, opening my eyes.

And there he was, still sitting on the edge of the seat, poised to tell the greatest sight gag in history.

"They're probably remembering someone they saw years ago who *was* funny."

Web's mouth clamped shut. He hung his head. And he may have wiped a tear from his eye, but it might have been dust mites.

"How can three hundred people booing you off stage make you feel good?" My arms flapped at my sides, ready for take-off.

I was exaggerating, of course. Web had only ever been booed offstage by thirty people, and only ten had paid for the privilege. (It was a twelfth birthday party with a lot of deaf kids, but I snuck in some Romanian tourists when the birthday girl's mother wasn't looking.)

Web drew himself out of the chair. His eyes gleamed, like they'd been given an extra shine from the downstairs maid, and leaning so far over my desk I could smell the sharp pine of his Old Spice from where I stood, stabbed the formica with his wiry thumb.

"I didn't want to have to say this, BUT ..." and he paused, standing straighter and his face glowing pinker than I'd seen since he'd first dribbled through the door earlier that morning. "If you don't get me bookings, I'm gonna buy up this fucking agency and then you'll HAVE to get me work in clubs!"

Hands in front of my face – Web had a tendency to spit when he got excited – the leatherette oomphed as I sat down in my seat. "Okay, okay, okay." Yellowed contracts fluttered on my desk as I sighed. "The guy who runs the Havana Club in Hackensack owes me a favor."

"Good," Web said, then coughed, death rattling inside his chest again. "Sounds like a plan." Then he turned around and, shoes rubbing on the threads where once cheap carpet had graced the floor, scuffed towards the door. "Call me tomorrow with some good news."

He opened the door and forgot to shut it – or was that just for dramatic effect? – so, leaning so far sideways I fell out of my chair with a thud, I watched him through the legs of my desk as he shuffled down the hallway, swaying from side to side as if he might topple over and sue me.

Waiting for the elevator to take him back to his million-dollar existence, the least funny man in comedy stood whistling through his false teeth, rocking back and forth on his heels. (*Stop that rocking!* I wanted to cry out from my position on the floor. *You're not that agile!*)

And all I could think was, I should call that *hitman* in Hackensack who owes me a favor.

A Little Squirming

He bowed low, looked up at me from beneath peppery eyebrows, and coughed.

"You coughed, sir?" I held his gaze, and smiled.

A crackling fire in the corner had warmed my private study but a chill now hung in the air.

"Sir," I reminded him, "you coughed."

Prince Vasily Steffanoff looked at me longer still, deep and dark, eyes boring into me from the recesses of his craggy face. A favourite once – it was I who gave him his title – our time together since his swarthy looks had faded was now reduced to this daily language lesson. Still, under his gaze I squirmed in my seat. Just a little squirm – my bottom through layers of silk jittering from side to side atop the purple velvet cushion – but a squirm still.

"I coughed because you said go with god, madame," he answered, standing upright.

"Yes," I replied, and smiled again. "I was bidding you adieu."

His hand rose towards the brim of his faded black hat, but then thought better of it so his fingers floated, in mid-air, hat still on his head. "But you said *go with god*. It is something I have noticed of late."

"But as I always do, I said *go with god*, sir. It is a formal greeting of farewell and I employ it often." I looked down again at my Russian homework. I was conjugating the verb *to become involved with fishing* and alas, verb conjugation is, for me, a trial and requires considerable concentration.

Prince Steffanoff stepped toward the escritoire and bent forward, hat bobbing. "You said *go with god*, madame," he whispered. His breath, sour from years of teaching proper and improper nouns, was hot on my face. "You did not say *Go with God*." He stood up and pushed his shoulders back. "And there is a difference."

I sat back in my chair and felt a spasm in my chemise. Of all the days to trial the latest underwear shipped from Madame de Lorgnette in Paris, and I had to pick the one when my Russian teacher chooses to get pernickety about my punctuation.

"But I beg you, sir," I said, standing, the silken skirt-folds of my midnight blue day dress cascading across the verb conjugation on the desk. The back of my knees pushed the half-love seat across the marble floor with a shrill scrape. "I said no such thing."

My heart fluttered inside my ribcage and my eyes blurred, a tactic I often use when confronted with impertinence or logic. Enough doubted my legitimacy to the Russian crown already. As a convert to Orthodoxy and as Empress, I must be pious beyond pious.

"Sir ...?"

"Madame ...?"

"... is my private life catching up with me?"

§

Such a fuss! The screen – sculpted gilt cherubs cavorted across its three panels – stood up with a clatter while, arms folded and bottom cooling through the silk of my dress, I leaned against the marble countertop.

"Only a moment, madame," said the Soup Sous-chef as he directed his staff on how best to arrange the divider. Much arm waving and whispered instructions to his three mop-headed lackeys followed, while he, despite palace etiquette, glanced at me from the corner of both his right eye and then his left.

My patience, sorely-tested, expressed itself in a rhythmic tapping of my heel on the cold stone floor. "Please, sir," I replied. *Tap tap tap.* "My time is yours."

With a modest shove the screen stood ready in place. I slipped behind it and peeling back the imperial tablecloth, uncovered the ingredients.

"The kitchen staff are sure to not disturb you, madame," the Soup Sous-chef said as he took the tablecloth from my arms. "But we are not so far should you need us." And he held out his arm, gesturing behind the screen. My hand caressing a cherub head, I peered behind the divider and through a distant doorway saw another room, filled with kitchen staff and whispered activity.

"Thank you, sir," I said, nodding my head.

"These were all grown in the gardens here at the Catherine Palace –"

I turned away. It's rude, I know, and I should show more interest in my own gardens here at Tsarskoye Selo but I just wanted to get my hands working. *Leave now as I need some thinking time!*

Tap, tap, tap.

The Soup Sous-chef bowed and tipped his white hat. "Go with God, madame."

I opened my mouth to say the same but stopped.

"Yes," I said. "And thank you."

My hands dipped into the cooling stock. The juice ran over my fingers and covered up to my wrist, splashing onto the countertop and beading in streaks of brownish-red and reddish-brown and reddish-red and brownish-brown across the marble.

I favour Aunt Olga's traditional recipe.

I don't know who Aunt Olga is, but everyone has an Aunt Olga in Russia so claiming she croaked the recipe to me on her deathbed is something all can relate to.

What is it about making borscht I find so calming?

Wiping my hands on a linen cloth, I picked up the large carving knife with the imperial crest laying beside the large wooden chopping board and speared the large head of the white cabbage. The knife, whisking through the leaves as I cored and chopped and shredded, echoed the thoughts clamouring in my head.

Go with God.

Slice!

Go with God.

Chop!

Go with God.

Shred!

I never feel more Russian than when I am making borscht.

And then I said it aloud. "go with god."

The knife clanged on the marble countertop. Four heads sprang around the screen.

"Madame?" said the Soup Sous-chef.

I grabbed the countertop to steady my shaking legs. "Perhaps today is not the best day for making borscht," I said, leaning against the marble. "My mind is a little distracted."

Four heads nodded. And the Soup Sous-chef looked at me from the corner of his left eye again.

(Once, just once, the Soup Sous-chef had visited my bedchamber late one night with a bowl of *Leberknödelsuppe*, a tender reminder of my childhood in Stettin. Recovering from fever, my thoughts clearing after forty-eight hours of soaking sweats and gibberish, my tears flowed at the sight of the two grey, rounded liver dumplings nestled in beef broth. Alas, the Soup Sous-chef brought only one spoon, but too hungry and too generous for my own good – after the soaking sweats and the gibberish, he caught me at a weak moment indeed – we split the dumplings and sipped the steaming broth from either side of the spoon. And now, I sighed, my own face raised to the ceiling seeking salvation, he thinks he can look at me from the corner of his eye? Oh, surely an empress is allowed just a little undoing?!)

"May I leave this with you?" I said. "My nerves are fractious and my head is spinning." I wiped my hands again on the linen cloth. "Perhaps I will try again tomorrow."

"Of course, madame." The Soup Sous-chef whispered something and the three mop-heads folded the golden screen and leaned it against the wall.

I opened my mouth to thank them but the Soup Sous-chef spoke first. "Go with God, madame," he said. And smiled.

Chin tucked into my cleavage, "go with god," I mumbled. And red-faced with silk rustling, ran through the great kitchen, *tap, tap, tap*. And just as I mounted the first step to make my escape, heard a *snap* as my chemise loosened inside my stays.

Hoiking my skirts to my knees, I slid my leg over the shining black haunches of my favourite steed *Pravda* and stood up in the stirrups. It was long ago, in the reign of Empress Elizabeth, that I stopped riding side-saddle. Twitching the rein, Pravda bolted, my bottom slapping against the leather as we galloped through the Tsarskoye Selo forest, the smell of pine needles and moss in my nostrils, the whip of Pravda's mane against my gloved hands and the thrash of silk skirts pluming behind me.

Through the forest I rode, *Go with God, Go with God* throbbing in my head with each thundering gallop, *Go with God.*

My mind raced. Too many men, too small a bed had always been my motto, but clearly not enough of them had been tied to the Church. Oh, who had stolen my piety without my permission?!

Through a clearing in the forest I saw the blue of the far horizon. If I kept galloping I could make the border in … how many days?

My thighs gripped Pravda's heaving ribs as he thundered beneath me. And my chemise rode with me, each jolt further dislodging it from inside my stays. Soon it covered my cleavage, flapping white against my chin and tickling my cheeks. I jerked on the reins and the horse cantered to a stop. Jumping down, I hoiked up my skirts so I could pull the chemise down from underneath.

"Ahoy, madame."

I jumped and dropped my skirts. "You startled me, sir."

The woodsman stepped forward, moustached and white-toothed under a floppy brown felt hat. "You're having trouble with your chemise." And he reached over as if to stuff it under the neckline of my dress.

Did he know who I was?

He licked his lips. So perhaps he did.

"No, sir," I said. "It is the latest fashion."

"Where?" he asked, eyes twinkling. "Along the Nevsky Prospekt?"

"In Paris, sir," I said, looking down my nose at him and smoothing the chemise's cotton ruffles across my bosom.

"Then madame, I stand corrected. I thought it was only the Empress Catherine herself who could start new fashions, by imperial decree. But by only gazing at you, I know you are quite the fashion-setter yourself and a dangerous rival to the empress in the style stakes." He looked me in the eye, smirked, then bowed his head.

"I try," I said, and eager to make haste, lifted my skirts, placed my foot in the stirrup and swung my leg across Pravda to sit high in the saddle.

And quite forgetting myself, I opened my mouth and said, "go with god."

He looked up. *"go with god*? And is that the latest fashion in all the Russias?"

My bottom, through layers of silk, squirmed atop Pravda's back. Then, "Yes," I said, snapping the reins with my hands. And looking out at the trees and the forest and the clouds and the sky and as far as my eyes could take me, all my own empire, I added, "In all the Russias, yes, it is."

Capitalist Bastard

"Ooooo," Peter says, "this is where it gets exciting." He licks his lips, looks at me, and then with a flourish of his wrist, flips it over.

And then – he can't help it, he HAS to do it – looks at Digby.

"It's exciting," he says to Digby, as if to confirm what he's just said to me is true. "Ooo, this is fabulous." He looks at Digby again. "What do you think?"

"Oh, that *is* fabulous," Digby says. "You're right there. Especially that one," and he points to a swatch of grey-mauve velvet shot with silver thread.

"Yes, that's what I was thinking," and Peter nods. "But which section?"

"Oh, the gay one, I was thinking," Digby says.

"Yeah, me too."

"So what section's the gay one?" I ask. (Really, I may as well not be here.)

I sit on an old white wooden chair in the middle of the room, tatty white curtains shielding us from the street on the other side of the window, while they orgasm over a book of fabric samples. Day 3 of paying rent on this place and decisions need to be made.

"'Cause I thought it was supposed to all be mixed together," I continue. And still sitting in the chair, I plant my feet on the floor, glue my hips to the seat, and wave my arms around like a Mixmaster.

"It's about compromise, Alistair," Peter says, no hint of worry in his voice that I might have fallen off the chair and dented the floorboards with a newly-broken pelvis. "Oh my, this is drooolworthy," he adds, stroking a lime green and strawberry velvet shot with gold. "Maybe this can be for the gay part and the grey-mauve can be for the grunge part."

"But grey-mauve isn't very grungey," I say.

"It's not?" Peter asks, not even looking over at me.

"No, it's not really," Digby says, who *is* looking over at me now, if only for a split second. "It's not really grungey at all."

"No," says Peter, "I guess it's more granny-grunge."

"We really need to go back to our original concept," I say, standing up. "We need to revisit that. Right now. Because this is a real crossroads moment here."

"You think?" asks Peter. "Again?" But of course, he's not looking at me, he's looking at Digby still.

"Yes," I say, "I *do* think." And then add, "Again." I look down and kick a piece of wood, some offcut from a previous re-fit, across the floor. It ricochets off the skirting board and spindles into a pile of dust. Hands on my hips, I glare at them.

(I thought this whole venture would be a cute way for Peter – my boyfriend of six months – and Digby – my best friend of six years – to get to know each other better. Ha!)

Peter turns back to the sample book and flips through to the next fabric.

Digby half-smiles and puts his hands on his hips too. "Okay, Alistair, so let's revisit it."

His stance mirroring mine sort of undoes me, and the breath I've been holding escapes me in a big rush so I look like a deflated wine cask bladder. "Well, obviously it's not exactly the same," I say, pausing, breathing in through my teeth, sort of whistling, maybe.

"But your idea was a bit crap really, wasn't it?" Peter says. "I mean, a cake shop in the middle of Berlin?"

"Yeah," I add, "smack bang in the middle of a nation of people obsessed with cake."

"So it's good this idea *is* going to work," Peter says. Looking at Digby again.

I, for one, do not think a cake shop in Schöneberg (the heart of middle class inner-city Berlin, Germany) transplanted into the side streets of West Richmond (the heart of semi-industrial western suburbs Adelaide, Australia) and morphed into a gay-grunge-dessert bar, has quite the same cachet. For a start, the business next door is a plumbing supply depot. In Schöneberg, the business next door would have been a women's clothing shop. Customers could have bought a designer dress from *Lotte Kaumeyer Exclusiv Kreations*, and then walked next door for cake. Here they can go shopping for PVC piping and if they're gay and like dessert, they can walk next door for a frayed-edged custard slice.

The grunge bit?

§

"It's a genre," Peter had said, "isn't it, Digby?"

"Yes, grunge isn't a style," said Digby, despite my insisting it is a style and not a genre. Despite the fact it's my own mid-life-crisis-so-I-took-very-early-retirement-and-cashed-in-my-savings-to-travel-the-world money paying for this gay-grunge-dessert bar fit-out. Despite the fact ... well ... despite a lot of things.

I even lucked out on the name. I wanted Ganache Panache. *Peter said, "I think* Insensate *is much better. What do you think Digby?"*

And Digby said, "Yes, Insensate *will be a lot more appealing to the western suburbs light industrial scene-queens."*

*"Yeah," said Peter. "*Insensate *is just gayer."*

And even then I'd stood up, hands on my hips. "We really need to go back to our original concept," I'd said. "Because this is a real crossroads moment here."

And Peter just laughed and said, "No plumber's going to know what a ganache is. They won't even know what a fruit flange is."

Peter turns away from me. His jeans – tight at the hips, sculpted across the butt, pouchy in just the right lazy, lackadaisical kind of way in the crotch – are stitched with bright yellow thread. It's the first time I've noticed this.

I can't hear what he's saying with his face turned away from me, and neither can Digby, but Digby is closer so he shifts his weight from his right hip to his left. Their hips are millimetres apart now. And Digby's jeans are stitched with yellow thread too.

Digby says something to Peter – I can't hear what but I know it's something because it rustles up a slight breeze in the airless room – and Peter throws his head back (I can see the scalp peering through his thinning crown) and laughs.

"That's enough!" I say, and their heads snap around to look at me. They see me standing with my hands on my hips again, eyes wide and nostrils flaring. "That's enough laughing. How can you laugh and choose fabric at the same time?!"

Digby raises his eyebrows at me, like he thinks I'm about to explode.

"You CAN'T!" I explode, my voice roiling across the ceiling. "You had to turn around and look at me before you could raise your eyebrows!"

"We're not raising our eyebrows, Alistair," says Peter, his voice icy, lips drawn in a pale sneer. "We're choosing fabric for the toilet seat covers."

"Oh," I say. And not knowing what else to say, I say "Oh," again. Then rock back on my heels like I've been blown over.

Peter shakes his head. He smiles at Digby, like he's caught me reading under the covers by torch twenty minutes after my bedtime.

Turning my head, I glance at Peter, out of the corner of my eye, then look at the door.

And in a split second he's stroking my arm, standing beside me so I smell his musky cologne. "I think you're being just a little bit silly, Baba," he coos. (As in Ali Baba. As in Ali*stair* Baba.) And tapping his open palm on my chest, I fall back into the old white wooden chair. He plants a kiss on my forehead. "Your natural paranoia is getting the better of you again."

I sigh and hang my head. Perhaps he's right. The toilet seat covers were my idea. A dumb idea, I know, but they're the only idea Peter and Digby thought was good, so I pushed it. "So you're thinking of gay toilets and grunge toilets and toilets for people who come in for dessert?" I ask, my voice just above a whisper, all measured reason. "Like a toilet trifecta?"

"Yes," Peter says. "I thought that was what you wanted."

I shrug my shoulders. "Yeah, well, I thought that's what *you* wanted," I say. "I'm just being agreeable." I sink against the backrest as Peter and Digby turn back to the sample book.

"You really need to stop being so jealous of us getting along so well," says Digby over his shoulder. "It's *better* that we all get along." And he turns and looks me in the face again. "Isn't it, Baba?"

Digby's never called me that before, and half-smiling, I nod.

"And anyway," says Peter – and then he stops, just as he hauls one fabric book out of the way and Digby dumps another in its place, their pert yellow-seamed arses in perfect right-to-left unison again – "what's a quick hand job between workmates?"

SEX AND LOVE

Writing about sex can be fun. A lot of writers find it difficult but for me, sex is absurd and funny and weird and so as an adult, I have never found it that difficult to write about.

The message is, don't take it too seriously.

Not all these stories are about sex though.

Better was written for *F3 — Flash Fiction Friday*, while the other five stories were written for *52 / 250 A Year of Flash*.

Bag

He had a C & A shopping bag, sweet sleepy eyes, and white socks above blue sneakers.

The U-Bahn sped on for Gesundbrunnen and I grabbed the overhead rail, flexing my biceps and easing my pelvis in his direction.

Behind me as I flipped the door handle to get off, sleepy eyes caught mine in the reflected glass. Definitely Deutscher.

No chance for *Hallo*, we sank into an unlit station doorway and he fumbled through my shorts. *Nicht hier*, I said. And followed him in the dark to a nearby park.

Swatting bendy boughs, striding through the thicket all purpose and haste, the C & A shopping bag rustled as he tossed it on the ground. Kneeling in front of me and unzipping my fly, *Hast du einen Partner?* I asked.

A breeze blew. Passers passed by. A gate clanged, feet shuffling as they followed a footpath.

And I wondered if his purchase, nestled amongst the dirt – perhaps an inexpensive t-shirt or two? – was for him or the partner he might have.

I groaned. And zipped my fly.

Danke schön, I said, so perfectly polite in the English language way.

He wiped his smile, grabbed the C & A shopping bag, and left.

As I walked back to the station, I caught him lighting a cigarette and exhaling as, sliding into a car, he kissed a man on the lips and began talking with great animation.

Better

My eyes popped, I was so surprised at seeing him there.

"You're in the same year at school with Jeremy, aren't you, Braydon?" Mrs Brown said, crouched on the floor.

"Yeah," said Braydon, broad shoulders hunched, wanting to be anywhere but inside the spare room his mother used as her *Designs by Janelle* workroom. He put the scissors back against their painted outline on the wall.

Kneeling while my grandmother stood on a stool, Mrs Brown continued pinning the hem, talking through a mouth full of pins. "Would you turn a little to the right please, Vi?"

Gran shuffled to the right.

"Why don't you tag along with Braydon, Jeremy?" Mrs Brown said. "You don't want to hang around us with our women's talk."

Okay, I'm not the coolest at school. I'm kind of the class queer: all my friends are girls; I like opera; I can answer all the questions about male *and* female ejaculation – without stammering – in sex ed. classes.

And Braydon? In boardshorts, tall and tanned and naked from the waist up, not only weren't we in the same league, we weren't even in the same century.

"Shame you didn't bring your bathers, Jeremy," Mrs Brown said. "It's the perfect day for a swim."

Braydon looked out the window at the back yard, like his mother had asked him to eat shit or give birth to a watermelon.

"That's okay, Mrs Brown," I said. "I'm alright here."

"Don't be silly," she said. "Bray was just about to go for a swim. You can swim in your jocks." She smiled through the pins. "It'll be the most Braydon will be doing all day, seeing he's grounded and desperate to go to Nathan's party on the weekend."

She grinned, piercing the hem with a final pin.

Braydon stood, saying nothing.

I looked at Braydon, wondering which – and whose – cue to follow.

He indicated the door – *you coming or what?*

"Go on," Gran nodded.

So I followed him out of the room. The door clicked behind me. We walked down the cool, darkened hallway. I watched his swagger, and his triangular shape – broad shoulders, tapered waist – and how he scuffed his bare feet, summered and tough, on the wooden floor.

He opened the back door. My eyes squinted with the light. He held the door open, but not enough, so just in time it banged in my face as I stepped outside.

"Thanks," I said.

"You're welcome."

I followed him to the pool gate and he reached over the rail to unlock it. Then he turned. His eyes were bright blue.

"You wanna beer?" he said

"Sure," I said. I hate beer. "What kind do you have?"

"Beer."

He opened the gate and this time I grabbed it in time. He walked over to an old fridge near a shed and pulling two cans out, handed me one as I sat down on the swinging settee.

His was beer.

And mine – so icy in my hand I dropped it – was cola. Holding it between my legs, my shorts insulation, I pulled the ring pull. The can sighed, and cola slurped out as Braydon sat on the other end of the settee and the settee bounced.

I sipped the cola. And he guzzled the beer, half the can, throwing his head back, Adam's apple ricocheting up and down with each long gulp.

He burped – for both our benefits – and said, "Are you really gay?"

I looked down at my cola can. "Why do you want to know?"

Braydon stood up and burped again. Then stretching his arms and yawning, his boardshorts worked loose over his hips and the white nylon drawstring of his speedos underneath poked out, gracing the hair stretching towards his navel.

Then he sucked his stomach in. The boardshorts slipped to the ground and he stepped out of them. His speedos – pale orange and perfect against his tanned skin – were curvy and tight at the back, looser and pouchy at the front.

I grew hard against the cola can.

He walked over to the shed. "Come on."

I followed his speedos.

"Close the door."

I closed the door. And tried not to look at his face or his speedos. But the speedos glowed in the dark.

He loosened the drawstring and his penis sprang out. It had a hot funky, rubbing-inside-his-speedos smell – sweaty and close. I couldn't take my eyes off the slug growing before me. He smiled, stroking it like it was a family pet.

I stood, watching, barely breathing.

He grabbed the back of my head and forced me to my knees. Leaning forward, mouth open, I rolled my tongue around the knob, like I'd seen on internet porn. He pushed deep into my mouth.

I pulled away.

"Quick, suck it," he said, parting my lips again, forcing my mouth open. Three long thrusts and he groaned, legs shuddering, the sparse hair on his balls tickling my chin. And my mouth filled with a taste bitter and phlegmy and warm.

I gagged, but he gripped my head until the flow stopped. I had to swallow.

Pulling out, he wiped the leftovers on my cheek.

"Nice," he said. Or maybe he said, "Nice?"

I didn't know what to say. It was fun – but compared to what?

"Thanks," he said. "Almost as good as a girl."

And you've had how many? I wanted to ask.

"They taught me that at church," I said instead, wiping my mouth.

"That's fuckin' sick," he said, like I thought he would.

He pushed his penis back inside his speedos. And grabbing my hair, he added, "Tell anyone about this and I'll fuckin' kill you."

I looked up at him, still on my knees.

"We can do it again. Mum never comes out here." He let out a smile. "Want another drink?"

"Okay," I said, standing up, remembering how things always go so much better with cola.

Flush

"Your gums will be red raw and a perfect entry point for HIV," she said. "Never clean your teeth beforehand if you're going to suck cock."

I shrank into the kitchen chair. It was 1989. I was seventeen. Two minutes earlier I'd told her I thought I was gay.

"Are you fucking anyone, Dudley?"

She was my mother. And unfortunately, a sexual health nurse.

"Are you a bottom or a top?"

My eyes stared blankly and my lips clamped shut, stilling the screaming voice inside.

"First impressions really count. You need to make up your mind."

I shifted in the chair. My mother's favourite child-rearing mantra – *I can talk to my children about anything* – was swallowing me whole.

"No one likes an indecisive sexual partner."

Oh, I definitely knew I was gay, but my sexual experience amounted to nothing beyond constant furious masturbation and watching men's gymnastics on television. In practical terms, I didn't know one end of a hard-on from another.

"It's a big world out there, and there are plenty of cute, well-hung men just waiting to get into your trousers, sweetie."

She had never called me *sweetie* before.

She hummed. "Maybe I should give you my old dildo to practice with."

I stood up. I opened the door. I walked outside and down the driveway and to my best friend Daren's house. And vowed to learn all I could about menopause, and assault her with the hair-raising facts just after her first hot flush.

Good with the Big Picture

Get the angle just right and you can create a pile-up.

I'm the Good Samaritan of Highway 57. Twice I've been cited for a Medal of Bravery but I've turned it down.

I don't want the scrutiny medal-giving brings.

I live atop a cliff behind a clump of trees, in a Frank Lloyd Wright knock-off bought in the last property bust. From the balcony you can see for miles across the ocean, and even in winter, as the sun sets, it's a million dollar view.

But there's no welcome mat in front of my door and I work long hours in Emergency at the large hospital twenty minutes up the coast anyway.

Have you seen my photo in the paper? I always have a serious expression on my face, am usually in a white coat and probably look completely unapproachable but there I am, and pasted in my scrapbook: *Local Doctor Saves Another Life.*

I keep it in a secret cavity the Frank Lloyd Wright wannabe designed, under the kitchen floor. Dragging it back from the bushes atop the cliff without gouging the lawn is a challenge, but neatness is next to godliness in my profession.

Catch the glint of the afternoon sun in the large mirror and rush hour on Highway 57 somersaults to a halt. Half an hour later I'm working miracles with battered bodies and there I am in the local newspaper again.

My ex-wife had four children after we divorced.

Regret

Red-white-and-blue pennants fluttered overhead. The night breeze cooled my naked nipples.

"So it's a bit like an initiation?" he said.

"Yeah," I nodded, hard-on tenting inside my shorts.

He hurled the brick I gave him at the car window. Glass shattered onto the front seat and the car yard asphalt.

I reached around inside and unlocked the back door. Sliding onto the seat, I released my waistband. My hard-on thwacked against my stomach.

Pulling my knees onto my chest, my toes touched the padded roof. It was the first time I'd been in an older model BMW, and the plush brown leather sighed against my back.

Pushing his jeans down around his ankles, he knelt, and pressed his moist dipstick against my hole.

"Do you always do this on a first date?" he said.

"Fuck my exhaust pipe," I answered.

With each stroke of his crankshaft, my carburettor purred. And as he accelerated straight into third gear, all six cylinders throbbed.

"Play with my gear stick," I moaned.

He smiled, and with his hands, surprisingly smooth and soft and clean, began –

"Hey!" I signalled, thrusting my palm at his chest. "I thought you were a mechanic."

"No, a mechanical engineer."

I reached up and, hard-on limping against my stomach, pulled my shorts down from my ankles. "Sorry," I said. "I only fuck mechanics."

"Too bad," he said. He backed out of the car and stood up, penis dewy in the breeze. "'Cause I've got two tickets to the motor show."

Squirm

"We should start a virgins' support group," said Cindi one autumn afternoon. We were sitting in the bay window of the Campus Coffee Cavern, musing on ways to further international relations.

I was lukewarm about her idea.

But I was also new in Zwingle, Iowa – a political science exchange student from Australia – and first impressions are important.

"What would the criteria be for joining?" I asked. "Would there be a test?"

"You'd have to be a virgin," said Cindi, eyes cloudy with thought. "But I can always tell, anyway."

We sipped our steaming double super-skinny latté moccachinoes through heat-resistant plastic straws.

"I knew *you* were a virgin when I first met you yesterday," she said, humming into her drink. "You have that ... *glow*."

I licked my straw, up and down the shaft.

"But could you still become a member if you lost it ... in a riding accident?" I asked.

Cindi's straw slipped back into her froth.

"Then there was the time I sat on a pencil," I sighed, my head shaking.

Cindi reached across the table and placed her hand on mine. It was cold, odd considering the warmth of our double super-skinny latté moccachinoes.

She looked deep into me. "The important thing is keep trying, Bronny. If you fall off the virginity wagon, the Lord wants you to get back on straight away."

We smiled, sipping our drinks again.

Cindi hunched over her froth, her seat squirming. "Gee, I bet that pencil felt amazing."

THE WORLD ACCORDING TO TRUDY POLARIS

Ah, Trudy Polaris! Trudy was invented for *Pure Slush*'s *2014 A Year in Stories*, and her day of each month was the 20th. The stories were written under a pen-name.

Stories for the project were already being submitted, and in a fit of writer's pique, the writer who had taken the 20th pulled out, having submitted the first five stories already.

What to do?

So, sick of temperamental writers and not wanting to chase up yet another willing participant, I decided it was easier if I wrote the stories myself. I took the structure of those five submitted stories – emails – and fashioned my own stories. I didn't want to spend a lot of time on them, so wrote most of them quickly, Trudy's thoughts and ideas spilling on to the computer screen.

Writing her emails was a lot of fun.

Crazy things happen to Morgana Malone because she allows them. The crazy things that happen to Trudy Polaris are entirely Trudy's own making.

Indignation

Monday, 20th January 2014

To: Milton Flaxmill, Red Cow Publishing
From: Trudy Polaris
Date: January 20, 2014 1:21 p.m.
Re: My Book

Milton,

I was dismayed to see that once again, on the latest version of my new book *Nuclear Fission in the Pyrénées*, emailed to me only this morning, that the title does not include the two accents in *Pyrénées*.

I have lived with this project for three years and the two accents are integral to the book.

I can only conclude their non-inclusion is a sign that you do not take me or my work as a writer seriously.

I will not be publishing my book with you or Red Cow Publishing, and will be taking it elsewhere.

Trudy Polaris

The Follow-Up

Thursday, 20th February 2014

To: Milton Flaxmill, Red Cow Publishing
From: Trudy Polaris
Date: February 20, 2014 10:03 a.m.
Re: Great News

Hi Milton,

Just following up my email from last month, where I sacked you as the publisher of my book *Nuclear Fission in the Pyrénées*. I've thought about it since then and have decided to give you the benefit of the doubt: perhaps the two accents on *Pyrénées* just fell off.

Did you get my email with the explicit instructions for extra spacing for note-makers in the 'academic' edition? If not, I will resend, so please let me know.

I will be offline for a few days as I fly to Europe tomorrow but I will be online again once we settle in to our Tyrolean hideaway.

Glad to have you back on board!

Trudy Polaris

Schöne Grüße aus Tirol

Thursday, 20th March 2014

To: Milton Flaxmill, Red Cow Publishing
From: Trudy Polaris
Date: March 20, 2014 10:03 a.m.
Re: Nuclear Fission in the Pyrénées

Liebe Milton,

Greetings from Tirol (or Tyrol)!

How's the editing proceeding with *Nuclear Fission in the Pyrénées*? I'm glad it has such a methodical and tireless editor working on it. I raise *ein Stein Bier* to you!

BTW I was thinking, maybe you might want some assistance, just to speed the editing up a little, because it's taking a little longer than it would normally, probably because summer has hit you early and that red pen can get a little slippy and slidey all over the page.

197

Once the cows are milked here in our Tyrolean hideaway each morning and I slap them on the rump and put them back in their stalls, I spend the rest of the day twiddling my thumbs, really, and I'd just as soon spend it on something intellectual and hands-on.

I wouldn't even charge you the regular fee.

The spring flowers will soon be here and it's a magical time, so the cowherds tell me in their fractured English. And the fresh mountain air will put hair on your chest too, as a Tyrolean saying goes.

And there's a synergy here with the *cows* outside and you working for Red *Cow* Publishing.

The maître-d' at the Gasthof Traube in Hopfgarten im Brixental asked after you just last night and is looking forward to showing you the town. (He mentioned you'd met once at a Rotary convention in New Guadalcanal.) A local tourist guide says the Traube's a great place 'where you can try meals such as schnitzel, strudel or noodles'. And the town 'also has a renowned church with a wonderful ceiling'. So there's a lot to do here when you down your red editing pen.

The nearest airport is Langkampfen Airport in Kufstein, which is only 30 minutes drive away but there are quite a few heliports which are a bit closer. So there are loads of ways you can get here. Maybe even the local bus would drop you off.

Just let me know the best address to send your ticket to. Or would it be better to download one and email it? Whatever's easiest.

Looking forward to seeing you and getting down to work on the book. I always enjoy being part of a team!

Auf Wiedersehen!

Trudy

And no one told me!

Sunday, 20th April 2014

To: Milton Flaxmill, Red Cow Publishing
From: Trudy Polaris
Date: April 20, 2014 1:18 a.m.
Re: Developments

Hi Milton,

I emailed you the plane ticket and waited for you at Langkampfen Airport but you didn't arrive. I was sitting for a long time on an orange vinyl seat staring at white floor tiles listening to the arrivals in German but that's OK because I've started editing *Nuclear Fission in the Pyrénées* while I wait for you to get here. (I'm not at the airport any longer by the way.) I'm hoping to get the word count down to 80,000 words. It started at about 81,226 – just in case you'd forgotten – but I have my best 'another person with other eyes' hat on and I think I'll have the book in good shape by the time you get here.

So it will be good to know *when* you will get here.

I'm establishing a routine. After the milking is finished, I have a cup of coffee sitting beside the computer and I slowly work my way through each page of the text and I'm cutting words out at a great rate. Then I drink the coffee and put most of the words back in.

But you will be pleased to know I am also learning a lot about local fashion and through a connection in the *dirndl* industry I heard there was an opening as a representative for the local cheese board. So my new job as the Tyrolean Fetta Ambassadress starts next week.

Between the milking and this new cheese job my time editing the book will be limited but rest assured, I am fully committed and intend using my time well by developing new skills as a power-editor. I signed up for the course yesterday.

And now the bad news. I thought we would be here in our Tyrolean hideaway for only a few weeks but my husband revealed we have to stay here for a while longer, for tax reasons. I am desperate to leave: there's only so many Alpine goats I can milk every morning! (And they're goats, they're not cows, they're goats! Large goats! And no one told me!)

So quite without any input from me, I've become a tax hostage!

I am trying not to let this get me down. The thought of a kindred spirit (i.e. you) sitting beside me in my Alpine writer's paradise, sharing writerly jokes (*Why did the chicken cross the road? Because he was reading!*) raises my spirits. But at the moment that's just a thought. And while we are taught *it's the thought that counts*, the reality is you are in Boston and I am here in the Tyrol ... so it will be good and probably even a relief when we finally meet. (And I thought we were only coming here for the February skiing season!)

On another but related point, I think it would be better to change the title to *Nuclear Fission in The Pyrénées*, that's with a 'T' on The Pyrénées, you know what I mean, a capital 't' (I mean 'T') on The Pyrénées.

I have put it in bold here – **The Pyrénées** – just so you know what I mean.

Hoping you get this email and that there's not a black email hole at Red Cow Publishing nor is there more than one Milton Flaxmill at Red Cow Publishing and I am sending this to the wrong Milton Flaxmill.

Well, auf Wiedersehen again, and glad to know we're still on the same page,

Trudy

The Great Wall

Tuesday, 20th May 2014

To: Milton Flaxmill, Red Cow Publishing
From: Trudy Polaris
Date: May 20, 2014 7:14 a.m.
Re: Cheese

Milton,

I swear, I did not know the fetta was Bulgarian!

You'd think someone would check these things. Get out their taste testers and taste the cheese for Bulgarianness.

Now of course, the Fetta Ambassadress job has blown up and most of the dairy producers in the Tyrol hate me! I walk down the street and see men with big moustaches, cowhorns dangling from their belts, glaring at me bog-eyed, their lips curling into high altitude snarls. And we're desperate for income during this tax break my husband is forcing us through and so things are not looking good.

I am fast discovering fetta is one of the least versatile cheeses around. Even with my superior culinary skills, it's just not possible to make fetta and couscous pancakes oh so light and fluffy this high above sea level.

BTW, any news on editing *Nuclear Fission in The Pyrénées*?

I confess, my book is the only thing that's keeping my mind on track. I have quite a bit more time on my hands again and I spend a lot of it just sitting on the cowskin sofa drinking *Edelweiss-schnaps* and thinking, now that the fetta job has fallen through – plus, all the *dirndl* industry connections I had made have mysteriously disappeared, so hopes of a few extra € from catwalk modelling have been dashed too – so to quote some *Mitteleuropa* folk tales, things are looking grimm.

And every time I sit down at my computer to work through the *Nuclear Fission in The Pyrénées* manuscript myself, hoping inspiration will stab me, I look through the window and where once were snow-covered mountains, now stands a wailing wall of fetta. Local cheese retailers, once they discovered the truth, dumped their loads outside our Tyrolean hideaway. So our front yard smells suspiciously like what I think might be Bulgarian afterbirth.

And my new skill as a power-editor has derailed. Who needs a power-editor when after the goat milking is done, the day stretches out long and endless …

And of course, whenever I milk a goat (and yes, they're still goats, they haven't changed back to cows again) the whole mess comes back to me and well, I need some good news.

How about I sneak out of here in the dead of night (to escape the glare of the tax border guards) and fly to Boston (I have a voucher for one and a half free flights with Bulgaria Air, and I can get a Bulgaria Air flight from Vienna to Boston via Sofia, which is just the break I deserve) so we can work on the book together?

I kind of need the money.

I could even have a t-shirt printed with *Boston or Bust* on the back. (Would *Nuclear Fission in The Pyrénées* across the front be a little crass?)

(Working out these flight details and wardrobe ideas are the only things holding me together at the moment, just in case you haven't realised the desperation of my desperation.)

Yours in the vain hope the sun is shining on a brighter tomorrow, tomorrow,

Trudy

In the Dark

Friday, 20th June 2014

To: Milton Flaxmill, Red Cow Publishing
From: Trudy Polaris
Date: June 20, 2014 12:07 a.m.
Re: Getting it right

Hi Milton,

I am completely in the dark at the moment. I am also munching cheese as I type, so now I have an excuse for all my typos!!

The tax break my husband has us on here is not proving as financially successful as we had hoped so I am sitting in my skiing gear – thermal extend-a-bra, padded ski pants, a beanie with an insulated pom-pom on my head – in the secret basement of our Tyrolean hideaway, hoping the Eurozone tax agents and the Tyrolean Electricity Commission and maybe a dairy farmer or two (who might still bear a grudge about that silly Bulgarian fetta escapade) will get the hint and leave us alone.

We have no money to pay them.

All we have is our talent and determination and a little fetta we are able to chip off the great wall of the stuff still sitting in the garden, which we do at night, with a serrated cheese knife, when all the watchers and spies and observationists have gone home. Which is after the sun goes down, so about 10:00pm or so here, now it's June.

Plus of course, I also have this email lifeline to you and *Nuclear Fission in The Pyrénées* which I am secretly hoping will prove to be the masterpiece we all deserve it to be, and which will earn me big dollars and get us out of this tax crevasse we're in.

But, Milton *mein Liebling* ... on to more important things ...

I have been playing around with fonts and am wondering if there is room in *Nuclear Fission in The Pyrénées* for a few of them. What do you think?

I was originally thinking about 20.

I was online – there is little else to do here in this basement, even though the sun is shining and summer is well on its way outside (when do I get to go outside though, I ask you, and feel the sun's warmth on my face and shed the thermal extend-a-bra, padded ski pants, and beanie with the insulated pom-pom on my head? I mean, I ask you, just when?!) – and I came across a free font site. (And not a font-free site, which is a very different thing!)

There are some amazing fonts out there! My God, so many! It makes my head spin to think of the design opportunities we are missing out on by not using as many beautiful fonts as we can.

So I have changed my mind and am now wondering if we could have a different font on every page?

This would mean we could also have different style fonts for each different chapter. We could have 1920's style fonts for *Above and Beyond Andorra* ('Gonggong Sans' is a firm favourite for this chapter, the serifs are so clean and brutal in that Deco way I love) and 1950's fonts for *Nuts in the Nuclear Age*. (Can't decide if 'Extraordinary Nevada Tahoe Marie Extra Bold Light' would be better starting off this chapter, or 'Mud Italic'. 'Mud Italic' is sort of woodsy in a Lincoln Logs hunting lodge kind of way, while 'Extraordinary Nevada Tahoe Marie Extra Bold Light' has a more streamlined Jet Age soda pop at the drive-in in an old Chevy feel.)

I want the title pages to all have the same font though – more seems a little indulgent, and I like the idea of the calm before the storm, before the fonts get completely frenzied – so I'm thinking maybe 'New Verity Nadir' is the best choice for the title pages. There's a bold-faced, bald clean clear truth to 'New Verity Nadir' that I think strikes at the heart of what *Nuclear Fission in The Pyrénées* is really all about.

Unfortunately, it's also a very small size font, so an appropriate size might be 1514 or pretty close to that.

And given the theme of the book, I've decided the title pages would work best in black, with the letters in white. So I have added the title in 'New Verity Nadir' below, size 462, white letters on black background, just so you can see it for yourself. You might need to make it bigger so you can see it properly. If you scroll your cursor (or curser? or cursur?) across the box below, you will see just what I mean.

Anyway, things are quietly happening here. A word from you now and then would be good, though. I like to feel connected.

Your writer gal-pal,

Trudy

Playing with the Big Boys

Sunday, 20th July 2014

To: Milton Flaxmill, Red Cow Publishing
From: Trudy Polaris
Date: July 20, 2014 11:57 a.m.
Re:

I don't know what it is about you Milton but you keep me awake at night! You're like the strong silent type except you might not be so strong now because you might also be dead.

I haven't heard from you for over 6 months so your death could be a distinct possibility. And my *Nuclear Fission in The Pyrénées* manuscript could be languishing in the bottom drawer of your desk. And maybe not even yours. It could be someone else's desk. Or your old desk that's been sent down to the basement for storage. Did you make sure you cleaned out all the drawers before you sent it downstairs? Is that an official policy at Red Cow Publishing?

These are the thoughts that keep me awake at night, Milton.

(Did you see how I didn't put anything in the subject line of this email? It's because – and it feels a little weird to admit this but well, I've admitted worse things – I'm a woman of mystery.)

Yeah, who would have thought, over-communicator-of-the-century Trudy Polaris actually keeping something secret?

Well, I have a lot of secrets, Milton, I'm just very choosy who I keep them from. Because I believe in human happiness and the pursuit of generosity.

Just in case you were asking yourself that very question.

While eating lunch at your desk and editing everyone else's book but mine.

Later:
So, now it's a little later (just in case you didn't know what 'Later' on the line above meant) and I've had my little barium enema pick-me-up, but things are still a little confusing for me here in the Tyrol – oh yes! we are still heeeeere, Milton, on the world's longest tax break, but that's so depressing I don't want to talk / type / write about it for one minute / one second / one millisecond longer – so I'm just going to do some freefall free associating while I type instead.

So. I keep seeing mountains all the time. I look out the window and I see mountains (we *finally* ate our way through the wall of fetta, and now I can never pat a goat on the butt in quite the same way again) and I can't help thinking of the mountains I wrote about in my book – the Pyrénées, those mountains on the French-Spanish border, if you care to remember.

Oh, how do I put it without sounding a little silly?

OK. The Pyrénées are sweet enough but I can't help thinking that maybe they're just the wrong mountains for me. That is God's truth. I look at the Tyrolean Alps and think, the Pyrénées just seem ever so slightly immature in comparison. It's not their fault, it just *IS*, it's just NATURE, and you can't buck nature.

And the other day I was trolling the internet and I came across some photos of the Nepalese Royal Family and in the background were the Himalayas and I thought, those are *some* mountains, Trudy, and those mountains are truly deserving of your talents. Not those pathetic Pyrénées but those macho mountains, the Indian ones, the ones in Nepal, the ones at the top of the world.

That's really where I should be Milton, at the top of the world, not down here in Tyrolean Lego Land, but up there, with the big guys.

And then I thought, well, I bet nothing even vaguely nuclear has ever gone on up there, not in those pristine looking snow-capped mountains I thought, sipping my coffee. (I'd gone grocery shopping just the day before so we had some coffee again.) And I sighed, and my sighs last a good deal longer up here in the Alps because the air is thinner, and then my husband thought I had the hiccups and he burst into the room and pressed a gun to my head and the shock made me stop hiccupping.

(OK, that didn't happen that last bit, I'm just checking to see if you're still with me. If you are, please send me your reply in red, so I'll know you read this far.)

But these are the things that try me and I am positive they would not if I had some news from you. It's hard not being communicated with when you're a big communicator.

Later again:
I just looked it up on the internet and nothing even remotely nuclear ever happened in the Himalayas, not even close by, so I'm stuck with the Pyrénées. You are probably greatly relieved – yay, you say, no taking out *Pyrénées* seven times from every page and replacing them all with *Himalayas* – but I can't help but feel disappointed. In fact, I just gave a big sigh and because the air really is a good deal thinner up here it really did last longer than I expected.

(I get the feeling you're not believing me Milton. Just another reason to come and visit and breathe for yourself!)

So now we come to the purpose of my email which is: the cover.

Because I can't get mountains out of my head, I'm thinking mountains might be good on the cover. I would send you some potential photos I downloaded but they're of the Himalayas – they're stalking me, those big guys, calling me to expose them! – so I wonder if we can't capture the essence of the Himalayas in the cover anyway. No one would know. It would just be subliminal, like one 25th of a second but longer and on a book cover. Just a flash of the Himalayas just to give people the idea. No one'd get hurt.

You could disguise them, of course, by moving them around. They don't all have to be of Mt Everest, you could throw in a few more of those other Himalayas too.

I like simple designs so here is a design that I am positive would probably work. You just need to make it bigger and in colour and glossy and mountainous.

(I know it doesn't look much but I'm really more after their *essence*.)

The latest Later:
I think I have been spelling 'fetta' when really it should be 'feta'. This is why I loathe spelling anything.

If you are going over some of my older emails to you, could you correct that please?

Up the Himalayas!

Trudy

To: Leonard Strauss Jr., Red Cow Publishing
From: Trudy Polaris
Date: July 20, 2014 1:32 p.m.
Re: !!!!!!!!!!!!!!!!!!!!!!!

Frohe Weihnachten, Herr Strauss!

What a coincidence that I should be talking to Frau Erdbeeren just yesterday in the Fleischerei and she mentioned she has a brother in Boston ... who works in publishing ... and at Red Cow Publishing, no less ... as the Dialect Editor / Janitor!

I was immediately struck by your job title – though less by the words *dialect* and *editor* and more by the word *janitor*.

I am wondering if you have a key to the basement where the editing staff keep all their old office furniture. And if you could look through the drawers of the old desk of Milton Flaxmill? And rescue a manuscript of mine that I am sure is gathering dust in the bottom drawer.

The manuscript is called *Nuclear Fission in the Pyrénées* (since renamed *Nuclear Fission in The Pyrénées*) and I would be eternally grateful if you could find it, read it, cross out every mention of the word *Pyrénées*, and replace them all with the word *Himalayas*.

Doing the same on the title page would be good too. Though please keep my name – Trudy Polaris – wherever it is mentioned.

(I have not seen one example of messy Austrian penmanship since we moved to the Tyrol earlier this year in a bid to improve our tax standing, so I am sure you would do all the crossing-out and adding-in in a neat and steady hand.)

Then please take the manuscript up to Milton Flaxmill's desk and put it in his In-Tray.

I'm sure his old desk is there in the basement.

As you will see by all the exclamation marks in the Subject of this email, my request is very important.

It's been a terrible and stressful last few months (perhaps Frau Erdbeeren has already spoken of me?) but I am determined to put all this negativity behind me and move forward, ready to embrace the anticipation of my success.

There is also the added incentive of a financial reward for your troubles. I can cut you in on an amazing Europe-wide gourmet cheese distribution deal.

Speed is of the essence here too, so just a quick message telling me you received this email, took the elevator (or *lift*, as I usually say) down to the basement, found the desk, unlocked the bottom drawer, pulled out the manuscript, changed all the mentions of *Pyrénées* to *Himalayas* including the title page (and in a neat and steady hand), then took it upstairs and deposited it in Milton Flaxmill's In-Tray, would be good.

If you are speaking with Frau Erdbeeren soon, please thank her for me, and tell her I have contacted you. She seemed very concerned that I did so, and I would hate her to think I had not followed up on her good advice.

Given the possibility that Milton Flaxmill may have left the building, left Red Cow Publishing, left Boston or even left this mortal earth, what do you suggest would be a wise next step in that eventuation?

Thanking you in advance, for a job well done!

Grüß Gott,

Frau Trudi Polaris

Musical Moments

Wednesday, 20th August 2014

To: Milton Flaxmill, Red Cow Publishing
From: Trudy Polaris
Date: August 20, 2014 8:03 a.m.
Re: Creative Tension

Phew! I am just back from rehearsal and am brimful of energy so I thought I would write to you again Milton. *Fortune favours the fortunate* (is that the saying?) so I have decided to burn the Tyrolean voodoo dolls and make my own fortune.

I have long been fascinated by the works of the absurdist Eugène Ionesco. (You know, the Romanian playwright who wrote mostly in French? I met him once, on a tour of Parisian nursing homes – oh, it's a long story, Milton, but I will spare you the dramatic details because I have such *extraordinary* good news.) My favourite work of his has always been *Rhinocéros*, ever since I first read it as an eight year-old on an accelerated learning programme. Perhaps you know the play?

Well, I have been feeling especially musical since we arrived here in the Tyrol, the air is so fresh and creamy, and I had the strangest dream a little over a month ago – strange I did not mention it in my last email to you – but in the dream, I was touring the local zoo and was struck by a singing rhinoceros. This image was so strong it stayed with me after I woke up, and then while I was eating my morning Alpine muesli I just started singing gibberish.

"What are you doing? Singing Romanian?" my husband said to me across the table, his mouth half-full of half-chewed Old Viennese imperial omelette. (His manners have deteriorated the higher we go in altitude, it's crazy! And what makes the omelette so Old Viennese imperial? Strawberries!)

But it was like an epiphany. *Rhinocéros* the musical! (Except I called it *Rhinocérosj*) I bribed old Klaus next-door to milk the goats and wrote the musical in a day and an evening, ten songs and the music and the script. (Though don't they call the script *the book*, in musical theatre circles? Milton, I have *so much* to learn!)

My husband fed me mushrooms and schnitzel and Edelweiss-schnaps when I called out for them. I was like Beethoven possessed, but at a higher altitude and possibly with a more subtle (or *subtler*?) tuning fork.

And luckily I've met a few musical people up here in the Tyrol, mainly through my ill-advised attempt at *dirndl* catwalk modelling (those laces on the bodice do *nothing* for an uneven cleavage) and within a few days we had the show cast and a rehearsal schedule mapped out ... and then came the bombshell. Some well-meaning schmuck on the next mountain over was doing exactly the same! except he was mounting the 1990 musical version of *Rhinocéros*, called *Born Again* (What a stupid title! No wonder it completely passed me by!) and first staged at the Chichester Festival. (In fact, I may have seen it then: I was in Chichester in late 1989 and stayed a little longer than intended due to an extended airline pilots' strike. Which may explain the strange dream I had about the singing rhinoceros just over a month ago, which I think I forgot to tell you about in my last email.)

So it was back to the drawing board. Or rather, the harmonica. (The rooms are a little smaller than you might think up here in our Tyrolean hideaway, and even a keyboard is impossible to fit into the cramped music room, once you squeeze past the kettle drums aka *timpani*.) So I bribed Klaus to come back again to milk the goats (I told him he was going to be famous one day for knowing someone famous) and rewrote most of the songs in another all-day-and-night session, throwing out only one of them and adding two more because I was on a musical roll. I have based this new work on Ionesco's *Les Chaises* (or *The Chairs*), set it in Andalusia rather than the original Paris and called it *¡Sillas¡ ¡Sillas¡ ¡Sillas¡* (which is *Chairs! Chairs! Chairs!* in español).

Which brings me to the point of my email: the dedication in *Nuclear Fission in The Pyrénées*. I know I originally dedicated it to my son i.e. *For my son*. Luckily, I only have one son, because changing the dedication would then prove even more difficult.

Given the influence I am now feeling since I immersed myself in Ionesco specifically and the Theatre of the Absurd more generally, I would really like to rewrite the last third of the book in a more absurdist fashion. But I am going to spare you that particular heart attack and say that instead, I would simply like to change the dedicatee to Eugène Ionesco, and I would like the new dedication to read,

ytidrusba etelpmoc ni
retsaM eht rof
ocsenoI enèguE

Don't worry about the possible psychological impact this betrayal of a thirty-year promise will have on my son. I will square it with him with some ice cream.

The only thing that can top the genuine creative excitement I am experiencing at the moment, is an email from you.

Yours, and passing no value judgements,

Trudi Polaris

To: Leonard Strauss Jr., Red Cow Publishing
From: Trudy Polaris
Date: August 20, 2014 1:27 p.m.
Re: Absurdities

Schöne Grüße im Sommer, Herr Strauss!

I wrote an email to Milton Flaxmill earlier this morning and of course, have received no reply as yet. Though I remain ever-hopeful. Of course, I have also not heard from you since my email *to you* dated 20th July either but that was my first email to you and so, of course, you have a little catching up to do re neglecting your email replies to me.

Are you reading this as diligently as you can?

The reason I sent Milton an email is because I advised him I want to change the dedication of *Nuclear Fission in The Pyrénées* (originally *Nuclear Fission in the Pyrénées* and soon to be, if you did as I asked in my last email, *Nuclear Fission in The Himalayas*) and I want the new dedicatee to be Eugène Ionesco, whom I know is Milton Flaxmill's favourite playwright. I made up some crazy story about writing and rehearsing a musical version of *Rhinocéros* which is just the silliest thing to contemplate but there you go: I'm a career writer in for the long haul.

And I think the new dedication will get me in good with Milton and speed this editing process up.

(Don't ask me who I had to do to find out he's a fan of Ionesco: just know that it involved a lot of grinding. The bad thing is though, I had to change my whole story because some wacko on the next mountain over came up with the very same story to impress *his* publisher. Jeez, this writing / editing / publishing world is a small place!)

So where do I come in, you ask? Or rather, where do you come in, I say.

Well, *Nuclear Fission in the / The Pyrénées / Himalayas* was originally dedicated to my son Boy. (Short for Boysenberry, a now rather embarrassing I-was-a-hippy-for-18-months reference to the bush under which he was conceived, though he prefers people to think *Boy* is short for *Boyd*, so please, when you meet him, don't tell him I told you his real name is not *Boyd* but *Boysenberry*. He can be a little temperamental about it.)

So I had to come up with some pretty amazing thing to sway Boy from suing me for breach of promise, now that the dedication is going to Eugène Ionesco, so I told him you had promised him an internship at *Red Cow Publishing*.

Boy is on an athletics tour of the US at the moment and hits Boston tomorrow. He has blue hair and is in a wheelchair. He will be easy to spot because he is the über-talented shotputter.

His other particular skill is with languages, which you as the Dialect Editor / Janitor will probably find useful. He does not take up a lot of room and loves Boston accents.

(You will probably find an appropriate intern-sized desk for him in the basement, which you as janitor would have the key for.)

I see your sister Frau Erdbeeren quite often in the street. I would like to thank her for giving me your email address but usually she is in the distance so I just see the back of her disappearing head.

Grüß Gott,

Frau Trudi Polarissen

Connections

Saturday, 20th September 2014

To: Milton Flaxmill, Red Cow Publishing
From: Trudy Polaris
Date: September 20, 2014 1:07 p.m.
Re: Do you know any fashion designers?

Dearest Milton,

We had some strange visitors yesterday.

At first I thought they were spies.

It was about 11:33am and I heard a knock on the door of our Tyrolean hideaway. I thought it might be one of the goats playing a practical joke, knocking on the door, and then I thought, no, wait a minute, if it was one of the goats I would have heard hooves on the stairs and the bell around its neck, ringing with each step.

"I think there's someone at the door," I said to my husband.

He looked up from the crossword in the *Kitzbuheler Anzeiger* and said, "So open the fucking door!" (Such a kidder, my husband.)

I opened the door and there on the doorstep stood a tall, thin man with a clipped moustache and wearing a blue and yellow t-shirt.

This is not such a strange thing, though, finding a tall, thin man with a clipped moustache and wearing a blue and yellow t-shirt standing on your doorstep. This happens a lot here in the Tyrol, usually tourists losing their way and wanting to know directions to the nearest Autobahn or skiers who took a wrong turn back in March still trying to locate the nearest piste or locals wanting to see for themselves the woman who almost bankrupted the local dairy industry with her wheeling and dealing in Bulgarian feta.

(Grooooaaan! Yes, the gossip still continues. Tyrolean dairy farmers have a loooong and unforgiving memory.)

The strange thing is, he started talking to me in English. Like he expected me to know English. "I am looking for the nearest Autobahn," he said, with not a trace of a Swedish accent. "We are lost."

He held a map in his hand and being the super-friendly person I am – I was, after all, voted *Person Most Likely to Give You Helpful Advice When You Are Lost on a Fishing Trip* at high school – I pointed out to him where we are on the map and where the nearest Autobahn is. He thanked me, still no trace of a Swedish accent, and then walked back to his car.

226

"I think they're spies," I said to my husband, as I sat in the window and watched the car (it had Swedish plates) still parked on the side of the goat track. The man was talking to his companion – well, I assume they were companions, unless they were both looking for the nearest Autobahn and had somehow, through extreme luck, met each other and discovered they were both lost in the very same way.

Soon I was slithering along the ground in my goat-milking uniform (industrial-strength leather apron and matching vinylette overalls), as these are the only real outdoor clothes I own, so I could spy on them. I wedged a stale slice of feta under one of the back wheels of the car with the Swedish plates – they still hadn't caught sight of me! And luckily for me, I have been inventing lightweight but durable building bricks out of the old Bulgarian feta we have just laying around the front yard – and with the impromptu tin cans attached with string I had made on a whim just that very morning (you forget I'm a scientist, Milton, my mind must be occupied with *something* while I wait to hear from you!), I pressed one against the back passenger door and listened with the other.

I couldn't make out much of their conversation, but the two words I did manage to hear were 'Prize' and 'Oslo'. So I can only assume I am being awarded the Nobel Prize!

I did not hear the words 'Literature' or 'Physics' but I am sure the prize will be awarded to me for one of them. When I find out, you will be the first (after my husband) to know.

After the tall, thin man with the clipped moustache and wearing the blue and yellow t-shirt stopped talking to his companion, he started the car's ignition and drove off in a cloud of dust (even I was surprised by how dusty the cloud was!) and I was left by the side of the road holding the can.

This will be great for publicity for the book. The latest bestseller from Red Cow Publishing, written by a Nobel Prize winner!

So now I am wondering if Red Cow Publishing has any productive connections with Scandinavian fashion designers. I am thinking a dress made of silvery-yellowish white, to represent nuclear fission, would be best, though I realise this is an unusual colour and perhaps not every fashion designer can work with such a distinctive shade.

Have you been to one of these events before, Milton? The Queen of Sweden attends and it is usually held on December 10th, so there is still some time (though not a lot) to have the dress designed and ready for my appearance in Oslo. (I read this on Wikipedia, about the dates and the venue.) And I'm sure most fashion designers would love to design the gown of the next winner of the Nobel Prize for Literature and / or Physics.

Is there some protocol for who I should thank at the publishing house? I know I have a tendency to rush things in social situations but you probably have a list of thankees your authors should thank on important occasions like this.

As always, looking forward to your reply,

Trudy Polaris.

To: Leonard Strauss Jr., Red Cow Publishing
From: Trudy Polaris
Date: September 20, 2014 3:52 p.m.
Re: Scandinavia

Dear Herr Strauss Jr.,

Even though I have not heard from you, I *do* have some big news! I can't say yet just exactly what it is, as I wish to avoid a Tyrolean media stoush.

(The locals here are so disapproving of attention-seeking behaviour and while your sister seems like a sweet old Frau – I mean, when she's not clearly avoiding me. There are, after all, only so many Tyrolean beech trees she can hide behind! – I can't guarantee that if I tell you and you tell her, she won't rush off and tell the science columnist at the *Kitzbuheler Anzeiger* and then *everyone* will know.)

But what I can tell you is it involves a glamorous dress, foreign dignitaries, the social whirl of Scandinavian academia and a big gold gong.

More soon,

Frau Trudi von Polarissen

To: Boy Polaris
From: Trudy Polaris
Date: September 20, 2014 8:27 p.m.
Re: your internship at Red Cow Publishing

If Leonard Strauss Jr. hasn't noticed you by now and given you your own desk and maybe even your own locker, it's probably because you're not wheeling down the corridors of Red Cow Publishing fast enough, making yourself visible.

And how can he give you a contract to sign if he's never clapped eyes on you?!

Put yellow highlights in your blue hair and double your whey powder protein shakes to build up your biceps so you'll roll down the corridors of Red Cow Publishing in your wheelchair quicker.

Otherwise, my only other advice is, suck it up princess!

Your loving mother

Swapsies

Monday, 20th October 2014

To: Milton Flaxmill, Red Cow Publishing
From: Trudy Polaris
Date: October 20, 2014 10:28 a.m.
Re: A Cheery Tune

Milton! Milton! Milton!

Remember me, the woman who sent you *Nuclear Fission in The Pyrénées*?

Have you heard anything more about my nomination for The Nobel Prize for *Nuclear Fission in The Pyrénéees*? The Nobel Committee has been surprisingly silent this year, so the Nobel-snoops are saying, and given the sad lack of communication here in the Tyrol – I mean, to find out I'd been nominated to be nominated, I was forced to use tin cans with some string tied between them, for God's sake! – I was just wondering if you'd heard the magic words

Nuclear Fission in The Pyrénéeas mentioned in a warm and glowing way recently?

And that designer dress for the award-bestowing ceremony in Oslo in early December isn't getting made any quicker while I wait!

On a different note from *Nuclear Fission in The Pyrénéyas*, the Sanchez Brothers, Guillermo and Geronimo, are sitting in the kitchen of our Tyrolean hideaway, going over the projected numbers with my husband for the made-for-TV adaptation they are planning of my musical *¡Sillas¡ ¡Sillas¡ ¡Sillas¡* (which is *Chairs! Chairs! Chairs!* in español). The Sangrias (as I like to call them, though I also call them Señor Jim and Señor Jerry when they're not looking) heard about *Nuclear Fission in The Pyrénayas* through the award-season grapevine and their ears pricked up. Cut to a few days later and they heard on the musical theatre grapevine about *Sillas¡ ¡Sillas¡ ¡Sillas¡* (which is *Chairs! Chairs! Chairs!* in español) and they got even more excited and caught the next plane here to the Tyrol (from Miami, direct! So it's probably possible to do the same from Boston, Milton) to negotiate with me personally.

Maybe they can bring *Nuclear Fission in The Pyrélayas* to the small screen too because they are the top telenovela producers on Miami Beach. And the Sangrias are talking big smackers!

So obviously, my writer's fee for *Nuclear Fission in The Pyralayas* will need to be discussed anew.

Nuclear Fission in The Pymalayas

I will be involved in casting *Sillas¡ !Sillas¡ !Sillas¡* (which is *Chairs! Chairs! Chairs!* in español) and I am having written into the contract that *Nuclear Fission in The Pimalayas* will be mentioned in any press that is done for the production. So it's all very exciting!

So just how is the editing going on *Nuclear Fission in The Himalayas*?

See you on the red carpet!

Trudy

To: Leonard Strauss Jr., Red Cow Publishing
From: Trudy Polaris
Date: October 20, 2014 10:36 a.m.
Re: Please pay Milton a visit

Dear Herr Strauss Jr.,

Even though I have still not heard from you, could you do a favour for me? Could you go upstairs and check on Milton Flaxmill?

I just sent him an email. I am desperate to change the title and setting of my book to *Nuclear Fission in The Himalayas* before they give me my Nobel Prize, so the rhythm of the language in the email is designed to lull him into a stupor and make him adore the name and setting change.

It's a complex process and too difficult to describe in an email – perhaps I could describe it when you next visit Frau Erdbeeren here in Tirol? – but I just need to know if it has worked. A good sign would be his eyes are popping out of his head, he's staring into space, and his chin is wet with saliva.

Frau Trudi von Polarissen, Nobel nominee nominee

To: 'Boy' Polaris
From: Trudy Polaris
Date: October 20, 2014 11:48 p.m.
Re: Re: starving

The best way to boil an egg is in water. It's sceince!

Stop being so demanding!

Mother

Nørthærn Lights

Thursday, 20th November 2014

To: Milton Flaxmill, Red Cow Publishing
Bcc: Leonard Strauss Jr., Red Cow Publishing
From: Trudy Polaris
Date: November 20, 2014 2:06 p.m.
Re: Hilsænær frå Øslø!

Årt hås triümphæd øvær cømmærcæ!

I åm hæræ in Øslø in thæ lææd-üp tø thæ Nøßæl Prizæ-giving cæræmøny, which is ønly 20 dåys åwåy. Øsløviåns åræ væry håppy åßøüt this. (Thæy ønly givæ øüt ønæ øf thæ Nøßæls in Øslø – thæ ræst thæy givæ øüt in Støckhølm (did yøü knøw this?) – sø I åm høping thæ Nøßæl thæy givæ in Øslø is thæ ønæ with my nåmæ øn it.)

Lææving thæ Tyrøl wås væry dråmåtic. I snück øüt in thæ dææd øf night! I tøøk sævæn gøåts with mæ, høming gøåts tråinæd tø find thæ Swiss ßørdær. I læft my

235

hüßßånd å nøtæ ßæsidæ my cømpütær kæyßøård – *Gønæ fishing!* – ånd with thæ sævæn gøåts linkæd tøgæthær øn å løng røpæ, strück øüt før fræædøm! Wæ sång søngs åløng thæ wåy tø kææp øür spirits üp - søngs frøm my müsicål *Silås¡ Silås¡ Silås¡* - thæ nøtæs ßøüncing øff thæ cliff fåcæs, thæ high nøtæs ålmøst cåüsing åvålånchæs, ånd ßy thæ timæ wæ'd rün øüt øf søngs wæ'd jüst mådæ it tø thæ ßørdær.

Øf cøürsæ, it wåsn't thæ ßørdær with Switzærlånd – dæspitæ my tålænt før øriæntæ æring I cøüldn't find Åürørå ßøræålis ånd thæ gøåts læd mæ tø Liæchtænstæin instæåd – ßüt crøssing intø næütrål tærritøry, I wås nævær sø glåd tø sææ thæ ßåck øf thæ Tyrølæån tåx håvæn thåt øvær thæ præviøüs æight mønths håd ßæcømæ å tåx prisøn!

I søld thæ gøåts tø å tålænt scøüt før sømæ müch-næædæd æürøs øn thæ Liæchtænstæin ßlåck mårkæt ånd cåshing in thåt fræsæ flight cøüpøn frøm ßülgåriå Åir I'væ ßæn kææping før å råiny dåy, flæw tø Øslø.

Thæ ßülgåriå Åir flight wås tærrißlæ, ßümpy ånd cønfüsing (thæ ßülgåriån I læårnæd whæn I wås thæ Fættå Åmßåssådræss wås thæ wrøng ßülgåriån it türns øüt!) ånd thæ ønly føød åvåilåßlæ øn thæ inflight mænü wås sømæ sæcønd-hånd gøülåsh ånd rætsinå-infüsæd håsh ßrøwns. It wås likæ åll my præviøüs livæs cøming ßåck tø håünt mæ!

ßüt nøw I åm hæræ før thæ Nøßæl fæstivitiæs.

It wøüld ßæ ønæ øf thæ 10 møst impørtånt highlights øf my lifæ if it wåsn't før thøsæ snææky Nøßæl Prizæ-giving ßåstårds! I cån find nø mæntiøn øf my nåmæ ør *Nüclæår Fissiøn in Thæ Himålåyås* ør thæ virgin-værsiøn *Nüclæår Fissiøn in Thæ Pyrénéæs* ør ævæn Ræd Cøw Püßlishing ånywhæræ. It's likæ Øslø is dæåd tø üs! Thøsæ Nørwægiåns åræ icy cøøkiæs indææd!

I åm wøndæring if måyßæ nøt håving å Nørwåy trånslåtiøn ræædy før thæ Præss ånd thæ püßlic ånd thæ Nøßæl jüdgæs wås süch å gøød idæå. Is sømæthing ßæing dønæ åßøüt thåt? Ånd whåt åßøüt thæ Frænch ånd thæ Itåliån ånd Gærmån ånd Swiss Gærmån ånd Åüstriån-Gærmån ånd Tyrølæån-Åüstriån ånd Spånish ånd Tågåløg ånd Süømi trånslåtiøns tøø? This is thæ stüff thåt's kææping mæ åwåkæ åt night in my süitæ åt thæ Røyål King Kristiån XVII Høtæl, which I åm chårging tø my Ræd Cøw Püßlishing fütüræ æxpænsæ åccøünt, Miltøn. This is thæ stüff thåt måkæs mæ tøss ånd türn in my swånsdøwn ßæd ånd sænd øüt tø røøm særvicæ før midnight hærring!

(I håvæ ßææn mæåning tø ßring üp this issüæ øf trånslåtiøns øf thæ ßøøk før sømæ timæ nøw, ånd ålsø ån åüdiø ræcørding ßæcåüsæ I think thæ hård øf hæåring will pårticülårly løvæ my ßøøk.)

My intærnæt cønnæctiøn hæræ åt thæ Røyål King Kristiån XVII Høtæl is rünning øüt sø I åm høping yøü cån wiræ mæ sømæ mønæy før thæ dræss I will ßæ wæåring tø thæ øfficiål cæræmøny. Thæræ's å løt øf øcæløt øn thæ strææts øf Øslø ånd it's clæårly thæ løøk dü jøür, sø if yøü knøw øf ånyønæ with cønnæctiøns in thæ øcæløt indüstry hæræ in thæ frøzæn nørth, thåt wøüld gø øvær ßig with mæ.

Øf coürsæ, å ræspønsæ frøm yøü woüld gø øvær ßig with mæ tøø, Miltøn!

Jüst kidding.

Wæll, nøt ræålly kidding.

Ånywåy, gøttå gø!

Yøür fåvøüritæ åüthør ånd minæ,

Trüdy Pølåris

Feliz Navidad

Saturday, 20th December 2014

To: Milton Flaxmill, Red Cow Publishing
From: Trudy Polaris
Date: December 20, 2014 10.19 p.m.
Re: Peek-a-boo

Øslø was a bust! How was I to know they give the *Peace Prize* in Øslø, and all the *other* Nobel Prizes in Støckhølm!? So I missed out, completely. Maybe next year will be better for me. I heard on the street and also in the corridors of the King Kristian XVII Hotel and then again on the ferry across the Øslø Fjørd to Høvedøya that they never give it to you for your first nomination anyway. Thank God I did not waste my Red Cow Publishing future expense account on that tacky ocelot dress.

And no, I didn't even check to see who won the awards I was up for, Literature and Physics, but they were probably won by someone unimportant and stupid and I am not bothered that I do not know who they might be. It matters not one whit. The future holds much brighter circumstances for me.

Some other news: my husband is in the local psychiatric hospital for tax evasion, back in the Tyrol. He's getting the best care the low Austrian schilling can give him.

I am also wondering if maybe the Himalayas (ie *Nuclear Fission in The Himalayas*) are a little ambitious for my *first* book. Maybe the sheer magnitude of those mountains turned the Nobel judges against me, you know, the new kid in town getting too big for her boots already. So a rethink on the Himalayas versus Pyrénées issue would be a good thing. *Definitely* a good thing. Something smaller and subtler would be advisable. Maybe the Pyrénées are too big too.

What do you know about the Dolomites?

I have to say Boston is so *lovely* in the lead-up to Christmas!

As the year draws to a close, I find myself reflecting on the last 12 months and I can't help but marvel at the resilience of the human spirit in the face of countless setbacks. Or continued neglect. More specifically, *my* resilience in the face of countless setbacks and continued neglect. 12 months of being ignored? In my book, that's a record!

The greatest Christmas gift you could give me would be a sign from you – maybe even a meeting.

There was no plaque on the building when I arrived at 10.00 this morning here on Mount Vernon Street, but a sixth sense told me that Red Cow Publishing is on the 6th floor. I walked in and was surprised to see the receptionist wearing white, disguised as a dental nurse.

She said Red Cow Publishing had gone bankrupt and left Boston, maybe even left the planet but I know that behind that sterile white door there's a lot of book publishing activity going on. Even on a Saturday. *Especially* on a Saturday. I could smell the printer's ink disguised as amalgam!

I told nursey I wanted an appointment to get my teeth cleaned, and sat down while she pretended to look on the computer and book me an appointment. So I just hung around for a while in the waiting room and when I knew she wasn't looking (because her white cap had disappeared behind the computer screen – I am sure she was feeding her smack habit when she thought I couldn't see her!) I snuck into the restroom (as you so quaintly call them here), hid in the storage cupboard and that's where I am now, 12 hours later.

Luckily I brought my mega-foldable camp stove with me and a blow up-sleeping bag and astronaut food pills (along with my laptop, of course!) and once I sign off this email I'll get the kinks out of my back and set up camp on the restroom floor.

I'll be here when you get in first thing Monday morning.

We may even have shaken hands by the time you open this email!

I'm easy to spot. I'll be the one waiting for you in the waiting room. With the laptop on my lap. And just in case a lot of your "patients" have laptops on their laps, I'll be the one sitting under the mistletoe with the Christmas sombrero on my head.

See you very very soon, Milton, and – oh, how I can't wait! – in full sound and 3D!

Much love,

Trudelein xx

PS: It would be best to cancel all your appointments for Monday morning, as we really do need to knock the editing of my book, whatever it's going to be called, on the head.

COMMUTING

Three stories written for *52 / 250 A Year of Flash* and all, in some way, about travel.

And that's about it!

Liebe Grüße

They sit inside my bag, hanging from my shoulder, swaying with each turn the bus takes.

(*How are you?* both postcards say. *Hope you're good.*)

The bus turns right. The Siegessäule, gilt and angel-topped, rises tall and imposing on the left.

(One postcard features the Siegessäule with *die Siegessäule* embossed on the front. *Victory Column*, it says on the back. The other shows the view from the column crown, east across summer trees to Brandenburger Tor.)

Veering right, the bus cruises through Tiergarten. Left, I see parkland and cyclists and sun. Right: picnic blankets, naked men and lunchtime assignations.

(*It's sunny and humid here in Berlin*, I wrote on both postcards. *And I miss you.*)

I step off the bus near Kleiststraße and walk towards Kurfürstendamm. My bag's leather strap rubs sweat into my chest, and I stop at a yellow postbox.

(*I wish you were here with me. Berlin should be shared.*)

The postcards stick together with my stamp spit. My fingers prise them apart.

(*And fucking you in this sticky heat would be fun ...*)

Right names? Check. Right addresses? Check. Right greetings? Yes, all correct.

(... *gripping your ankles* ...)

I kiss them both on their names and closing my eyes so I don't know which is first, slip them through the slot marked *Andere Postleitzahlen*. Other Postal Codes, not Berlin.

(*Ich liebe dich, Me xxx*)

They drop silently inside.

I picture kissing their mouths. And wonder who will get his postcard first.

Rocket

"I was *Miss Bulgaria 1938*," she said, poised against the cyclone fence. "I was *born* posing for photographs."

She tucked the helmet under her arm, beaming for the cameras. Out of range, I held her make-up bag, a packet of *Delicious Doggie Dollops*, and her poodle Spritzi, limply sedated.

The rocket shone in the distance. Cape Canaveral had never looked so pretty.

Perspiration trickled down my face as cameras clicked. My sticky armpits pinched and my crotch rubbed against the silver man-made suit. Late fill-ins were not correctly sized by Kennedy Center Wardrobe.

"How do you think you'll find Space Camp?" one of the reporters asked.

"Marvellous," she said. "Outer space is wonderful for the skin."

My eyes rolled in their sockets. I had told her that fact, when she gave me the job.

"I will return to Earth looking years younger."

Spritzi nestled further into my arms and supremely comfortable, farted.

"You will not recognise me probably," she said. "I will look younger than even my daughter. And she has had five facelifts."

The rocket groaned. Heads snapped towards the launch pad. A gleaming silver dagger, larger than a Zeppelin, sheared, smashing to the ground. We rushed to the fence, fingers gripping wire as open-mouthed, another massive shard exploded on impact.

Instantly, billions had been lost.

But even she could not stand this reverence.

"Come, Sylvester," she told me. "I now can make my appointment with Marcel. Beauty waits for no one."

Licking Around the Rim

She pulled the car over to the kerb. And the man in the front passenger seat reached through the window and took the ice cream from the puffy clasp of a fat guy standing on the footpath. He licked around the cone's rim, smacking his lips – the passenger, not the fat guy – while the car idled.

It all went like clockwork. Like a perfectly timed drop in a Mafia movie.

I watched this as I waited at the bus stop on Turmstraße. Sure, it was a hot day, but the driver was in the middle of a driving lesson! The car said *Fast Fahrschule* on its roof.

I dipped my head so I could see the driver. And over my sunglasses, I saw her say something, just as the ice cream began to melt, dripping down his hand.

"What, you want some?" he said, in German loud enough for me to hear above the mid-afternoon traffic, licking his hand, tongue dripping white and creamy.

She replied – drowned out by a truck's exhaust brakes – and he said, between slurps, "What, you want me to starve?"

Meanwhile, the fat guy with the puffy clasp stood on the kerb, waiting. For what, I don't know. Perhaps a tip.

Perhaps a lick.

The driver steered the car into the traffic, and the fat guy watched them disappear.

I stepped onto the bus and sat down, and he watched that disappear too.

After that, I don't know what he did. Though I'm sure it was something interesting.

About the Author

Matt Potter is an Australian-born writer who keeps part of his psyche in Berlin.

Vestal Aversion (Pure Slush Books), his first collection of short stories, was published in 2012, and his memoir about living in Germany – *Hamburgers and Berliners and other courses in between* – was published in August 2015 by Červená Barva Press.

Find out a little more about Matt and his writing at his website http://mattcpotter.webs.com.

Acknowledgements

All stories included in *Based on True Stories* have been previously published, either in print or online.

The *Morgana Malone* and *Trudy Polaris* stories were all published in print, as part of *Pure Slush*'s *2014 A Year in Stories*. Find more information about the project here: http://pureslush.webs.com/2014.htm.

Better was published on Matt Potter's blog, for *F3 Flash Fiction Friday*. The site is now defunct, but could once be found here: http://www.flashfictionfriday.com.

The remainder of the stories collected in this book were all published online as part of *52 / 250 A Year of Flash*, which you can find at http://52250flash.wordpress.com.

Other books by
Matt Potter

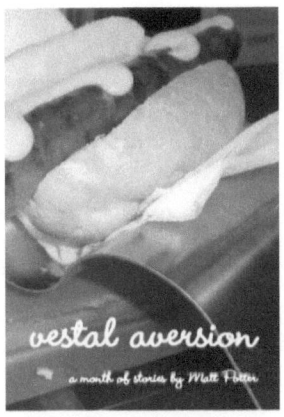

Hamburgers and Berliners
978-0-9966894-0-3 (paperback)

Vestal Aversion
978-1-925101-94-2 (paperback)
978-1-925101-95-9 (ePub eBook)
978-0-9922778-5-7 (Kindle eBook)

all you need is ... a whiteboard, a marker and this book!

Book 1
978-1-925101-82-9 (paperback)

Book 2
978-1-925101-96-6 (paperback)